TARGET FOR DEATH

Capt. Jack Boxer glanced at the sonar display. The killer darts were heading straight for the starboard side of the *Shark*.

"Come to one zero degrees," he ordered.

He keyed the Diving Officer. "Reverse dive . . . Reverse dive . . . Make one thousand feet."

"Roger that," the DO answered.

Boxer looked at the sonar display and switched on the ship's intercom. "All hands . . . All hands . . . We're going to be hit . . . Hold fast!"

Suddenly a sledgehammerlike blow struck the starboard side of the *Shark*. Boxer was thrown against the Command Computer.

Another sledgehammer blow struck the *Shark*.

Boxer sucked in his breath and waited for the explosion. . . .

THE SURVIVALIST SERIES
by Jerry Ahern

Available wherever paperbacks are sold, or order direct from the Publisher. Send cover price plus 50¢ per copy for mailing and handling to Zebra Books, Dept. 1769, 475 Park Avenue South, New York, N.Y. 10016. DO NOT SEND CASH.

DEPTH FORCE #5

— BY IRVING A. GREENFIELD —

ZEBRA BOOKS
KENSINGTON PUBLISHING CORP.

ZEBRA BOOKS

are published by

Kensington Publishing Corp.
475 Park Avenue South
New York, NY 10016

First printing: February 1986

Printed in the United States of America

One

The crew of the *Shark* was absolutely silent. All engines were stopped. Tight lipped, Capt. Jack Boxer sat at the Command Computer and watched the Digital Depth Readout Device. They were passing through seven five zero feet.

The Sonar Officer keyed Boxer. "Target bearing two eight degrees . . . Range one thousand yards . . . Speed three two knots . . . And closing fast."

"Roger that," Boxer answered in a whisper and checked the Sonar Display on the COMCOMP. The Russian cruiser, *Tallin,* was still bearing down on them.

Suddenly the bone chilling pinging of the cruiser's sonar sounded through the *Shark.*

Boxer keyed the Electronics Officer. "Activate ECM," he ordered.

"ECM activated," the officer answered softly.

The pinging stopped. But it would start again as soon as the Ruskies readjusted their sonar gear.

Boxer's gray eyes checked the DDRO. The *Shark* was nearing one thousand feet. Boxer keyed the Diving Officer. "Going from auto-dive control to manual . . . Making fifteen hundred feet," the DO responded.

"Target," SO reported, keying Boxer, "bearing four four degrees . . . Range twenty five thousand yards . . . Speed three zero knots."

"Roger that," Boxer answered and looking up at the sonar display, he saw the second blip near the edge of the scope. He pressed several of the COMCOMP keys. A moment later the *Tallin*'s specs came up on the General Info. Screen.

GUIDED MISSILE CRUISER—KARA CLASS
Displacement .... 9,000 tons
Length .... 574 feet
Propulsion .... gas turbines, speed 32 knots
Main Armament
  ..... 2 quad SS-N-3 ASW launchers
  ..... 2 twin SA-N-3 SAM launchers
  ..... 2 twin SA-N-4 SAM launchers
  ..... 2 twin 76mm DP gun mounts
  ..... 4 single 30mm Gatling guns
  ..... 1 KA-25 Hormone helicopter

Boxer rubbed his beard. The 'Copter extended the *Tallin*'s range and certainly gave it a considerable ASW capability.

"Skipper," the SO said, "the second target is *Krivak One*."

"Roger that," Boxer responded. He knew the ship. A whole class of guided missile frigates took their name from it. The ship was the most heavily armed of its type afloat. It was designed to hunt and kill submarines.

Suddenly the pinging started again.

Boxer put the *Krivak*'s name into the COMCOMP and activated the fire control switch.

An instant later the screen above him displayed the problem. A red light began to flash and across the bottom of the screen the words *NO SOLUTION* appeared.

Boxer turned to Cowly, his EXO, and said, "The FC gives me a 'no solution' response."

Cowly came close to the COMCOMP. "That sure as hell doesn't say much for our chances."

6

"Skipper, coming to fifteen hundred feet," the DO said, keying Boxer.

"Roger that," Boxer answered. "Stand by to level off."

"Leveling off," the DO said.

Boxer watched the bubble in the level indicator come to a null.

"Dive completed," the DO said.

"Roger that," Boxer responded. He turned to Cowly. "If that's the game," he said, gesturing with his head toward the COMCOMP screen, "then I want to at least take one of those Ruskie ships with us." He spoke matter of factly. "If we can get one of them, we might be able to survive." He keyed the Engineering Officer. "Flank speed," he ordered.

"Going to flank speed," the EO answered.

"Mahony," Boxer said, keying the helmsman, "switching the helm to manual . . . Come to course seven nine degrees."

"Helm over to manual . . . Coming to seven nine degrees," the helmsman answered.

Suddenly, the *Shark* shuddered from the hammer-like blow of an explosion above it; then another one astern.

"All stations, report damage," Boxer said over the MC.

One by one the reports came in negative.

"Helmsman, change course to one five degrees," Boxer said.

"Coming to course one five degrees," Mahony answered.

Another explosion shook the *Shark*.

"Helmsman, come to course—"

Thunder exploded above the *Shark*'s stern, forcing it down.

"Come to course one two five degrees," Boxer finished. Before he could ask for a damage report, the Damage Control Officer reported there was none.

The pinging stopped.

Boxer keyed the EO. "Stop all engines."

"All engines stopped," the EO answered.

Once again the *Shark* was silent.

Boxer uttered a ragged sigh, wiped his sweaty brow with a handkerchief, and leaning back, he stretched. The hours of sitting at the COMCOMP had tightened his neck and shoulder muscles. He was a tall, lean man with flecks of gray beginning to show in his beard and hair.

"Skipper," the SO said, keying Boxer, "The *Tallin* is dead in the water."

"Roger that," Boxer answered; then to Cowly he said, "The usual dip and sprint routine."

"The 'Copter worries me right now more than she does," Cowly responded.

Boxer nodded.

The SO keyed Boxer. "Second target changing course . . . Coming to bearing one five five degrees . . . Range ten thousand yards . . . Speed two eight knots."

"Roger that," Boxer said, glancing up at the sonar display.

"Soon the two of them will be on top of us," Cowly said.

Boxer didn't answer.

"Target," the SO reported, "nine zero degrees . . . Range two thousand yards . . . Speed . . . Speed . . . Target dead in the water."

"Roger that," Boxer answered; then to Cowly he said, "Sonar buoy."

"Target," the SO reported, "bearing one two zero degrees . . . Range one thousand yards . . . Speed . . . Target dead in water."

"Roger that," Boxer answered.

Suddenly the pinging began again.

"Helmsman, come to course four five degrees," Boxer said.

"Coming to course four five degrees," Mahony answered.

Boxer keyed the Launch Officer. "Standby to launch minisubs," he said.

"Roger that," the LO answered.

The pinging became fainter.

Boxer keyed the DO. "Come to five zero zero feet."

"Roger that," the DO said.

The SO keyed Boxer. "The *Tallin* is underway again . . . Bearing one three six degrees . . . Range one thousand yards . . . Speed three two knots."

Boxer acknowledged the report.

"Coming to five zero zero feet," the DO said.

"Ten four," Boxer answered.

The pinging became louder.

The SO keyed Boxer. "Multiple targets . . . Bearing eight four degrees . . . Range fifteen hundred yards . . . Speed—Skipper, they're making more than one hundred knots."

Boxer hit the klaxon button three times. "Dive," he shouted over the MC. "Dive . . . Dive!"

The hiss of escaping air filled the *Shark*. Its bow went down.

Boxer's eyes were riveted to the Sonar Display. Four targets passed over them.

"What the fuck was that?" Cowly asked in a choked voice.

"Vargas to the bridge," Boxer said over the MC. "Vargas to the bridge, on the double."

Suddenly the *Shark* was shaken by two explosions: one above and one below.

"ASROCS," Boxer said.

The DO keyed Boxer. "Passing through one thousand feet."

"Come to twelve hundred," Boxer answered.

"Roger that," the DO said.

Within minutes, Vargas came to the bridge. He was a short, wiry, dark complexioned man. He commanded the *Shark*'s assault team.

"Blindfold Borodine, his EXO, Viktor Karenski, and Doctor Suslov," Boxer said, "and bring them to the bridge."

"Aye, aye, Skipper,"Vargas answered.

The DO keyed Boxer. "Leveling at twelve hundred feet."

"Roger that," Boxer answered.

"Multiple targets . . . Bearing six two degrees . . . Range eight five zero yards . . . Speed ninety knots . . . Depth eight zero zero feet . . . Closing fast."

"Can you give me their attack angle?"

"Negative, skipper."

Boxer glanced at Cowly.

"Range seven five zero yards," the SO reported.

Boxer keyed the DO. "Make one thousand feet."

"Roger that," the DO answered.

Immediately the *Shark*'s bow began to rise.

Boxer keyed the helmsman. "Come to course two five five degrees."

"Coming to course two five five degrees," Mahony answered.

"Targets slowing," the SO reported. "Speed seven zero knots."

"Roger that," Boxer answered. Drawing his arm across his brow, he took a deep breath and slowly exhaled.

"Targets repositioning themselves," the SO reported.

Boxer looked up at the Sonar Display. The targets had fanned out in a line. "Christ," he exclaimed, as four more targets appeared on the screen.

"Another set of multiple targets," the SO reported.

"I have them on display," Boxer acknowledged. The targets were five hundred yards in front of the *Shark* and

10

closing fast.

"Leveling at one thousand feet," the DO answered.

"Dive," Boxer exclaimed. "Dive!"

The hiss of escaping air filled the *Shark*.

"We're at flank now," the EO answered.

"I need as much as you can give me," Boxer answered.

"Roger that," the EO answered.

An explosion suddenly rolled the *Shark* to its portside and another hammered down on its stern. The lights dimmed; then brightened.

The Damage Control Officer keyed Boxer. "Pressure drop in secondary water line," he reported.

"Roger that," Boxer answered.

"Repairs underway," the DCO said.

Boxer switched on the MC. "Section chiefs report injuries."

"Passing through one thousand five hundred feet," the DO answered.

"Roger that," Boxer answered. "Level at two thousand."

"Ten four," the DO answered.

One by one the section chiefs reported that none of their men was injured.

Boxer checked the Sonar Display. The two groups of multiple targets hadn't changed their course. The *Shark* was below them and still diving.

Vargas returned to the bridge with Borodine, his EXO and Dr. Suslov.

"Remove their blindfolds," Boxer ordered.

"Aye, aye Skipper," Vargas answered.

Boxer waited until their eyes became accustomed to the light before he said, "Unless I have your help Comrade Captain, none of us stand much of a chance of surviving."

Suslov's jaw went slack. Her eyes opened wide.

The SO keyed Boxer. "Multiple targets . . . Bearing

11

three four degrees . . . Range eight hundred yards . . . Speed nine zero knots . . . Closing fast."

"Roger that," Boxer answered; then, pointing to the Sonar Display, he said, "You can watch them up there. We've been dodging targets like them for awhile. We've been lucky."

"We refuse—" Suslov began.

"Captain," Borodine said, "the *Sea Savage* was sunk by those killer darts. There isn't any effective countermeasure. They are a new weapon."

"Targets on our heading," the SO reported. "Speed one zero zero knots."

Boxer glanced at the sonar display. The killer darts were heading straight for the starboard side of the *Shark*.

"Helmsman, come to one zero degrees," Boxer ordered.

"Coming to course one zero degrees," Mahony answered.

Boxer keyed the DO. "Reverse dive . . . Reverse dive . . . Make one thousand feet."

"Roger that," the DO answered.

Boxer looked at the Sonar Display. He switched on the MC. "All hands . . . All hands . . . We're going to be hit . . . Hold fast . . . Hold fast . . ." He turned to the Russians. "On the deck. Flat on the deck."

Suddenly a sledge hammer like blow struck the starboard side of the *Shark;* then the explosion followed. Boxer was thrown against the COMCOMP. Cowly and Vargas fell to the deck. Another sledge hammer blow struck the *Shark*. Boxer sucked in his breath and waited for the explosion.

The DCO keyed Boxer. "Starboard ballast tank number five ruptured . . . Section eight, starboard side taking water . . . Foreign object lodged in outer skin of starboard ballast tank three . . . Emergency pumps activated."

"Roger that," Boxer answered.

The DO keyed Boxer. "Heading to one thousand feet slowed."

"Will you be able to complete?"

"Affirmative," the DO answered.

"Roger that," Boxer answered.

The EO keyed Boxer. "Skipper we've lost one zero knots."

"Give me what you can," Boxer said.

"Roger that," the EO answered.

Boxer turned his attention to the Russians. "Then there is no defense that you know of?" he asked looking at Borodine.

"None.'

"Then the only thing I can do is play this hide and seek game until I run out of luck," Boxer said, speaking calmly. He was anything but calm.

"You could surrender," Suslov said.

Boxer shook his head. "I could, but I won't," he answered.

"You mean you'd have all of us die—"

"It is your people who would have all of us die," Boxer answered. "They're the ones who are attacking us."

The SO keyed Boxer. "Two sets of multiple targets . . . Bearing one nine degrees . . . Range six hundred yards . . . Speed nine zero knots . . . Targets closing fast."

"Roger that," Boxer said and looked up at the Sonar Display. Eight killer darts here heading toward the *Shark*. This time he couldn't risk diving to get below them.

"Target speed increased to one zero zero knots," the SO reported.

Boxer keyed the helmsman. "Come to course three two degrees."

"Coming to course three two degrees," Mahony answered.

Boxer checked the targets. They were changing their

13

course. He switched on the MC. "Stand by," he said. "All hands stand by for additional hits." He motioned Borodine and the others to lie flat on the deck.

The first explosion violently shook the *Shark*. The lights went out; then came back on. A second explosion smashed down on the stern.

Instantly a series of red lights began to flash on the COMCOMP.

The DCO keyed Boxer. "Two fires aft . . . Heavy smoke."

"Roger that."

"Two banks of air scrubbers cut."

"Roger that," Boxer answered.

"Skipper," the DO reported, "leveling at one thousand feet."

"Hold that," Boxer said; then switching on the MC, he asked all section chiefs for a casualty report.

"Two men dead in the stern torpedo room," the TO reported. "Three suffering second degree burns."

Boxer acknowledged the report.

The DCO keyed Boxer. "Skipper, the fires are out but the smoke is beginning to drift forward. One bank of air scrubbers is back in operation. The second bank has been badly damaged."

"Roger that," Boxer said. "Do the best you can with smoke."

"Ten four," the DCO answered.

Boxer turned to Borodine. "We've got one of those killer darts lodged in the outer skin of our starboard side."

"Your only hope is to surface and surrender," Suslov said.

Boxer looked at Borodine and said, "You tell her, Igor."

"Tell me what?" Suslov said.

"The *Shark* can still fight," Borodine answered.

14

"She is doing more running than fighting," Suslov answered haughtily.

"I could do no more than Comrade Captain Boxer is doing to keep his boat alive," Borodine told her.

"To keep us all alive," Boxer said, "I must find some way of countering those killer darts."

"Hide," Borodine said. "You could hide."

"You can't do what I think you intend to do!" Suslov exclaimed.

"We're all dead if I don't," Borodine answered; then to Boxer he said, "there is an undersea cave—"

"Where?"

"In order to show you, I need a chart of the ocean to the east of us," Borodine said.

Suddenly the dreaded pinging sounded through the *Shark* again.

"Christ!" Boxer swore.

The SO keyed Boxer. "Multiple targets . . . Bearing six two degrees . . . Range two thousand yards . . . Speed nine zero knots . . . Depth six zero zero feet and closing fast."

Boxer keyed the DO. "Make one thousand five hundred feet."

"Roger that," the DO answered.

"Helmsman," Boxer said, "stand by to change course."

"Standing by, Skipper," Mahony answered.

Boxer watched the approach of the killer darts on Sonar Display. They were closing very fast. With the sweat pouring out of him, he waited. When the killer darts were fifty yards from the *Shark*, he almost shouted. "Helmsman, one eight zero degrees!"

"One eight zero degrees," Mahony answered.

The *Shark* began to turn.

The killer darts were less than twenty five yards from the *Shark*.

Boxer sucked in his breath and watched the Course Indicator. The *Shark* was coming to one hundred and eighty degrees.

He raised his eyes up to the Sonar Display. The killer darts were passing; they were moving away from the *Shark*.

Boxer exhaled slowly. Every muscle in his neck, shoulders and arms ached. He shook his head. He was responsible for what was happening. Had he not rescued Borodine and his crew from the *Sea Savage*— He stopped himself from thinking about the things he shouldn't have done. He didn't have the time to look at the past. Now, only the present mattered. Sometime in the future, if he and the others aboard the *Shark* had a future, he'd take time to think about the past.

"The chart you wanted, Comrade Captain," Boxer said, pressing a series of keys that displayed a portion of the Pacific Ocean on the Map Display Screen.

"May I step forward?" Borodine asked.

Boxer nodded.

Borodine moved closer to the COMCOMP and looked at the map. "Here," he said, "at latitude ten degrees South and longitude one hundred seventy five degrees, twelve minutes East. There is supposed to be an undersea cave—"

"At least get something in return," Suslov said.

Borodine glanced at her; then looking at Boxer, he said, "I ask for nothing, Comrade Captain."

Boxer nodded. Despite the fact that Borodine had attempted to take control of the *Shark*, he felt an enormous respect for the man; even more, he genuinely liked him.

"That cave will give you the protection you need," Borodine said. "Before we diverted to—"

"You sunk the—"

16

"'Tried to," Borodine said. "She sunk us with the killer darts."

Boxer looked up at the Sonar Display. The two surface ships were still following the *Shark*. Boxer guessed the two 'copters were dropping more sonar buoys. He switched on the MC. "Now hear this . . . Now hear this . . . All hands . . . This is the captain speaking . . . We're going to make a run for it . . . We're going down to the bottom and hug it while we run . . . We've got some damage and we might not be able to run . . . But it's our only chance." He switched off the MC and keyed the DO. "Take her to within five zero feet of the bottom."

"Making two thousand feet," the DO said.

"Roger that," Boxer answered.

"Helmsman, come to three six degrees," Boxer said.

"Coming to course three six degrees," Mahony answered.

Boxer checked the speed. The *Shark* was doing thirty knots. He keyed the EO. "I'm reading three zero knots," he said. "Can you give me any more?"

"Negative, Skipper," the EO answered.

"Ten four," Boxer responded.

The SO keyed Boxer. "Multiple targets . . . Bearing seven seven degrees . . . Range six hundred yards . . . Speed nine zero knots . . . Closing fast."

Boxer looked up at the Sonar Display. The killer darts were angling in at the *Shark*.

Boxer keyed the DO. "Blow all tanks . . . Bow planes up one five degrees."

"Blowing all tanks . . . Diving planes up one five degrees," the DO answered.

The *Shark*'s bow went up. The rest of her started to rise.

Boxer switched on the Under Water Imaging System and watched the four killer darts slam in the rock seabed.

17

For an instant the picture on the screen showed nothing but swirling water. Then, huge chunks of rock tumbled through the water and crashed against the sea floor.

"All hands hold tight," Boxer said over the MC.

Moments later the *Shark* was tossed hard to its port side by the advancing shock wave.

"Stand by," Boxer said, "there's another one coming!"

The *Shark* seemed to drop off to the starboard, pitched violently from side to side and finally came to an even keel.

Boxer looked at the depth gauge. They were passing through the one thousand foot level. He keyed the EO. "Reduce speed to one five knots."

"Going to one five knots." the EO answered.

"All hands stand by to surface," Boxer said over the MC. He turned to Cowly. "When we come to the three hundred foot level launch our minisubs. I want them on radio control."

"Aye, aye, Skipper," Cowly answered.

"Have our 'Copters standing by for launch. Have them armed. They're to attack the 'Copters; then go for the ships."

"Anything else?"

"Ready the forward torpedo room. I want all tubes loaded and ready to fire. Ready the SS tubes. Have the missile crews ready for battle stations the moment we surface."

"Aye, aye, Skipper," Cowly answered and immediately began to implement Boxer's orders.

"You mean you're going to fight it out with our ships?" Suslov asked.

"If I don't," Boxer answered, "I don't stand a chance of bringing the *Shark* home."

"But—"

"Comrade Captain," Borodine said, "if they box you

18

in with those killer darts, you won't be able to escape."

"That's a chance I'll have to take," Boxer answered. "Sooner or later, I'm going to be hit and hit badly if I continue to run."

Borodine nodded.

"I'm going to have to ask you to leave the bridge," Boxer said.

"I understand," Borodine said.

Boxer summoned a junior officer and ordered him to escort Borodine, his EXO and Suslov back to their quarters. "With any luck," Boxer said, "we should be able to at least visit the cave." Then he turned his attention to the COMCOMP and the launching of the minisubs.

"Passing through three hundred feet," the DO answered.

"Roger that," Boxer answered and keying the Launch Officer, he said, "Prepare to launch."

"Standing by, Skipper," the LO responded.

Boxer checked the reading on the COMCOMP. The two subs were on radio control. One was targeted for the *Tallin*, the other would circle to draw fire from either ship. "Launch subs," he ordered. On the TV screen he watched the launch bay doors open and the two subs leave the bay. "Cowly," Boxer said, "you have command of the minisubs."

"Aye, aye, Skipper," Cowly answered. "Command signal go."

Boxer keyed the forward torpedo room. "Stand by to fire torpedos one through four."

"Torpedos armed and ready," the TO answered.

Boxer checked the *Shark*'s speed. She was doing twenty eight knots. The loss of the minisubs had given her an additional knot and a half.

Boxer switched the UWIS on. The water was clear enough for him to watch the progress of the minisubs.

They were two hundred yards in front of the *Shark* and moving at top speed toward the Russian ships.

"Skipper, they've targeted one of the minisubs," Cowly reported. "Taking evasive action."

Boxer keyed the forward torpedo room. "Putting in target info . . . Set responder to receive changing coordinates."

"Responder set," the TO answered.

"Stand by to fire."

"Standing by."

"Fire in sequence." Boxer ordered.

"Firing in sequence." the TO answered.

The bow of the *Shark* rose slightly then settled back. Boxer checked the Sonar Display. The *Shark* would surface a thousand yards to the sterns of the Russians.

"Minisub on target," Cowly reported. "Now."

On the Sonar Display Boxer saw the two blips merge. Moments later a thunderous explosion rolled over the *Shark*.

The SO keyed Boxer. "Target . . . Bearing six four degrees . . . Range one thousand yards . . . Dead in the water."

Suddenly another blip merged with the stationary target.

Within moments a second explosion came thundering through the water.

The SO keyed Boxer. "Target turning . . . New bearing one nine eight degrees . . . Range eight five zero yards . . . Speed three five knots."

"Roger that," Boxer answered. He checked the depth gauge. They were one hundred feet down and still moving up. He keyed the 'Copter launch bays. "Stand by to launch," he said.

"Standing by," the pilots replied in unison.

"Will recover you as soon as possible," Boxer said.

"Ten four," each of them said.

"Launch control switched to COMCOMP," Boxer said. "Launch in one zero seconds . . . Count down started . . . Stand by." He watched the hands of the launch clock race through an arc of ten seconds. A green light came on. Boxer keyed the COMMO. "Stand by to make contact with our flyboys."

"Standing by," the COMMO answered.

"Making surface," the DO said.

Boxer switched on the MC. "Surfacing . . . Surfacing Missile detail stand by."

The *Shark* broke water.

Boxer touched the klaxon once.

"Flyboys on radio," the COMMO reported.

"Roger that," Boxer answered.

"Minisub targeted," Cowly said. "Taking evasive action."

The Missile Officer keyed Boxer. "Missiles detail on deck . . . All missiles armed and ready."

"Roger that," Boxer said. "Targeting missiles from COMCOMP data."

"Ten four," the MO answered.

"Stand by to fire," Boxer said. "Fire!"

The roar of the missiles reached down into the *Shark*.

"Minisub destroyed." Cowly reported.

"Roger that," Boxer answered.

Boxer had targeted two of the six missiles for the *Tallin* and the other four for *Krivak*.

"One birdman down," COMMO reported.

"Antiaircraft crew topside," Boxer ordered.

"Two hits on the *Krivak*," the MO reported.

"Cowly," Boxer said, "take the CONN; I'm going on deck."

Grabbing his helmet and flak jacket, he hurried on deck.

The *Tallin* was listing to the starboard and burning. Smoke was pouring from the stern of the *Krivak*. But she was still maneuverable.

The Radar Officer keyed Boxer. "Target . . . Bearing two five degrees . . . Range two thousand yards . . .

Altitude nine hundred feet . . . Speed one five five knots . . . Closing fast."

Boxer keyed Cowly. "Switch AA to radar control . . . Set fire to commence instantly."

"Roger that," Cowly answered.

COMMO keyed Boxer. "Simmons got one of their birds."

"Ten four," Boxer said.

"He's going after the *Krivak*."

"Negative," Boxer answered, just as the multiple barrel AA gun opened up.

"Say again," the COMMO said.

"Negative . . . Have him stand by to ditch."

"Roger that," the COMMO answered.

The Russian 'Copter came roaring down on the *Shark;* then suddenly it became an orange ball. An instant later the ball exploded and pieces of it fell into the sea.

Boxer turned toward the two burning ships. The *Krivak* had pulled close to the *Tallin*. Now both ships were dead in the water. The fight had gone out of them. The *Shark* was saved.

Two

Boxer returned to the bridge and switched on the MC. "Mister Vargas, send two men topside to recover Simmons." Then turning to Cowly, he said, "As soon as Simmons is aboard, we'll stand down from GO. Have our mess people make up something special."

"Aye, aye Skipper," Cowly said with a nod.

"Keep her on the surface. I want to put some distance between us and the Ruskies before a repair crew goes over the side to see if we can get rid of that killer dart in our hull."

Cowly slapped his forehead. "Would you believe I forgot about that mother," he said.

"So did I," Boxer admitted, "until a moment ago." Then he added, "I'm going to send a report of the action to Langly; then I want to talk to Comrade Captain Borodine."

"Too bad he's on the other side." Cowly commented.

"That's the way I feel about him too." Boxer said. He scanned the instrument readings on the COMCOMP: they were normal.

He left the bridge and went to his own cabin, which was nothing more than a small room, with a bunk bed, a desk and miniversion of the COMCOMP.

Boxer sat down at the desk. He fished a pipe out of his

23

pocket, carefully filled the bowl, and then lit up. The smoke tasted good. For a moment, he closed his eyes and thought about going to sleep before taping his report. But then he decided to do it while the events of the last few hours were still fresh in his mind.

Even while taping, Boxer realized that Kinkade, the Company Chief, would be in his usual state of distemper after he heard the tape, and he'd immediately order the *Shark* back to Norfolk. But Boxer had no intentions of returning to his home base before he had a look at Borodine's undersea cave.

Cowly keyed him. "Skipper," he said, "we have Simmons off the port bow. We're stopping all engines to pick him up."

"Ten four," Boxer answered and continued taping. A half hour passed before he was finished. Then he brought the tape to the Communications Room and told the COMMO to, "encode the tape to a priority ten and send it simultaneously to Langly and the Chief Of Naval OP, Admiral Stark."

"Aye, aye, Skipper," the COMMO answered.

Boxer nodded, and leaving the CC, he went directly to the mess area where Borodine and his crew were held.

As soon as one of the Russian sailors spotted him, he called the others to attention.

Boxer nodded and said to Borodine, "Comrade Captain, have your men return to what they were doing."

Borodine said a few words and the men relaxed.

"May I have a few words with you, Comrade Captain?" Boxer asked.

"Yes, though first I want to tell you how much I admire the way you managed to save the *Shark*. Naturally, I cannot congratulate you for what you did, but it would be less than true if I pretended not to admire the way you did it."

Boxer suppressed a smile and said, "In similar circum-

24

stances you would have done the—"

Borodine held up his hand. "Those were the words I was going to use to explain why I agreed to try and take the *Shark* from you."

"Command is command," Boxer answered.

Without speaking for several moments, the two men looked at each other; then Boxer said, "I'm going to take the *Shark* to the cave."

Borodine nodded. "I had no doubt that you would."

"I would want you on the bridge," Boxer said.

"Doctor Suslov, or any of the other scientists would be more valuable than myself."

"I'll ask her," Boxer said. "But I'm certain that she'll refuse."

Suddenly Boxer's beeper sounded. He switched on his communicator.

"Skipper," Cowly said, "Simmons' aboard."

"How is he?"

"Fine. He says the *Tallin* will probably sink."

Boxer glanced at Borodine; his face was expressionless.

"Ten four," Boxer answered; then to Borodine, he said, "The game we play is a deadly one."

"Only to those who die," Borodine answered.

Again neither man spoke for several moments; then with a nod Boxer said, "Next time in Paris, or wherever else we happen to meet, we'll drink a toast to the men of *Tallin* and the *Krivak*. And, if you are agreed, have a mass said for them."

"I wondered if you believed," Borodine said.

"I don't," Boxer answered. "But it was the only gesture I could offer in addition to toasting them."

"I look forward to our meeting," Borodine answered.

"Now to the business at hand," Boxer said. "In a circumstance like this, have you the authority to order Suslov to help?"

"No," Borodine responded.

"Then I will—"

"She might be willing, if you made an attractive offer."

Boxer raised his eyebrows.

"She would not want to be interrogated by your people, nor would I."

"Do you think I'd let that happen to you Comrade Captain? Once we are finished with the cave, I intend to locate one of your merchant ships and put all of you aboard. I didn't save your lives to turn any of you over to my people. I saved your lives because I believed it was the thing to do. I also believed that if the situation were reversed, you would have done the same thing."

"For us there is no other way," Borodine said. "But if you want her help, you must offer her something in return—something she would want very, very much. Strike a bargain with her for the thing you were going to give her of your own free will."

Boxer clapped him on the shoulder. "There's a lot of devil in you, isn't there?"

"I suppose there is," Borodine answered, smiling broadly. "And in you too."

"In me too," Boxer answered.

Then the two men began to laugh so hard tears came to their eyes.

Three

Bruce Kinkade, director of the CIA, was a man of middling height, stubby fingers and a bald pate. He sat rigidly in front of Admiral Stark's desk. Stark, tall and lean, was Chief of Naval Operations.

"I came here because—" Kinkade started to say; then stopped. He and Stark had their differences, none the least of which was Captain Jack Boxer. "I thought it best to ask you to order Boxer to return to base."

"I have already done that," Stark answered in his gravelly voice. "And I have received a reply from Captain Boxer." He handed a piece of paper to Kinkade.

"Mission not completed," Kinkade read aloud. "What mission?" he questioned, his voice rising in proportion to his mounting frustration and anger. "The Ruskies are going crazy. The *Tallin* was damaged so badly, she had to be sunk. The *Krivak* was so badly damaged she had to be taken in tow."

"According to Boxer's report," Stark said, "the Ruskies fired first. He was forced to defend himself."

"He provoked the attack."

Stark was tempted to reach for a cigar but, in deference to Kinkade's recent heart attack, he decided to forgo the pleasure.

"He has taken prisoners—"

"Hold it right there!" Stark exclaimed. "Borodine and

27

his crew are not prisoners aboard the *Shark*."

"Initially they weren't," Kinkade agreed. "But once they attempted to seize the *Shark* and, by force of arms defeated, then they became, by any standard you choose to apply, prisoners."

"And you want them?"

Kinkade nodded. "The information they could supply would be invaluable to us and to your people."

Stark pursed his lips.

"You know I'm right," Kinkade said. "And you know as well as I do that Boxer will not return with them."

"Probably not," Stark admitted.

"I want them. Your people should have a crack at them."

"I have already ordered Boxer to return," Stark said.

"Cancel the mission."

"I can't cancel something I know nothing about," Stark answered.

"You have the authority to do it."

"I have," Stark answered, "but I know if Boxer is doing something, he has a good reason for doing it."

Kinkade was silent. Hard as it was for him to admit it, he nodded; then he said, "The trouble is that his 'good reasons' so often come in conflict with mine. We both know he's not going to turn Borodine over to me."

"I don't think he will."

Kinkade shook his head. "I don't understand his kind of patriotism. It's something he's invented for himself, like his relationships with women."

"Doesn't every man invent his relationships with women and have his own idea about patriotism."

"By God no! Most men accept what society—"

"Boxer isn't most men. None of the men on the *Shark* are. They are unique, or they wouldn't be on that boat."

Kinkade shook his head. "My own granddaughter thinks he's some kind of a god. Trish—" He stopped himself. "I'm sorry I brought a personal matter into the conversation."

"I'll give you that Boxer isn't an easy man to put up with," Stark said, "but whatever faults he has, lack of patriotism isn't one of them."

Kinkade leaned forward. "If either you or I were in his place, we'd bring the Ruskies back. I would and I'm sure you would. But he won't."

Stark pressed his hands together and then separated them and asked, "What do you want me to say?"

"What can you say, other than what you have already said?"

"There's nothing subtle about our brand of patriotism. But with Boxer—"

"I swear, if he didn't cause the Ruskies so much difficulty, I'd almost be able to convince myself—and probably a number of other people—that he was a double agent, or if not that; then certainly a strong sympathizer."

"I don't doubt that you'd be able to," Stark answered. "Congressman McElroy—"

Kinkade shook his head. "Without the photographs and tapes of Trish and Boxer, McElroy would have destroyed him."

Stark agreed. "But," he added, "there were the photographs and tapes. Now, from what I hear, McElroy has become the leader of some weird political group and he doesn't stand much chance of being reelected."

"The group is called, 'Americans for an American World.' McElroy is the founder and president of the organization. His financial support comes from such diverse sources as farmers and working people throughout the country and—"

"Loonies with money to give away," Stark said.

"Not to mention several very large corporations," Kinkade added. "So far, it's all very harmless."

29

Stark gave a disdainful snort.

"That sums up my feelings about it too," Kinkade said. "But it's a free country."

Stark nodded.

"Well," Kinkade said, "I tried. You're the only one who could bring the *Shark* back. I surely can't."

"Boxer will bring her back," Stark answered.

"But without the Ruskies."

Stark smiled. "Better to have the *Shark* and her crew back, than the Ruskies."

Kinkade stood up and Stark did the same.

"I'm seriously thinking of retiring," Kinkade said. "I'm getting too old for this job."

"I know what you mean," Stark answered. "Just the other day I was thinking the same thing. But it was one of those days where nothing went right."

"There have been all too many of those lately," Kinkade answered, offering his hand to Stark.

"We'll go down to the pier to welcome Boxer when—"

"Trish will insist on being there too," Kinkade said.

"There's no reason I can think of why she shouldn't," Stark said.

Kinkade dropped his hand, turned and walked quickly and quietly out of Stark's office.

The *Shark* was directly over the area where the cave was located. The outside bridge was up, and from it Boxer was watching a DEMO team remove the killer dart lodged in the *Shark*'s outer skin.

The work was delicate, requiring a small circular portion of the hull be cut out with a torch. Then the killer dart was carefully placed in a rubber assault boat and taken two hundred yards off the port side, where the DEMO team began the dangerous work of defusing the missile.

Boxer keyed the team's section chief. "Any snags?" he asked.

"Not yet, Skipper," the man answered. "Lucky there's no time delay on it . . . just an impact fuse."

"Roger that," Boxer answered, looking down at the place where the missile had been removed. Another team of men from the Damage Control Section was already welding a patch into place.

The DEMO team chief keyed Boxer. "Two wires to cut—"

Suddenly there was an enormous explosion and a tall thin column of water erupted from the ocean's surface and immediately fell back.

Boxer's jaw went slack. He switched on the MC. "Emergency Recovery Team topside, on the double . . . Emergency Recovery Team topside, on the double!"

Vargas came up to the bridge and looked over toward the floating bits of rubber.

"Don't think there's anything left of the men," Boxer said tightly.

"Sharks!" Vargas said, pointing to the right of the debris in the water.

The Emergency Recovery Team's chief keyed Boxer. "Team standing by, Skipper."

Boxer switched on the MC. "Shark alert," he said. "Shark alert." Then he keyed the EO. "Give me enough turns to ease the *Shark* about two hundred feet."

"Ten four, Skipper," the EO answered.

Boxer turned to Mahony. "Get us as close as you can," he said to the helmsman.

"Aye, aye, Skipper," Mahony responded.

The *Shark* began to slide through the water.

Boxer keyed the EO. "Stop all engines."

"All engines stopped," the EO answered.

Men with high powered rifles equipped with telescopic sights were already on deck and had sighted on three

31

of the five sharks.

Boxer signaled them to fire. Two of the sharks were hit and one was killed. The men fired another volley. Three sharks bellied up!

Boxer keyed the Emergency Recovery Team. "See what you can bring back . . . It's too deep to dive here . . . Anything you find will be on the surface."

"Roger that," the team chief answered.

An instant later four men went over the side.

Boxer watched them slice through the water.

"Sharks . . . Sharks . . . Three points off the starboard bow!" a junior officer on the bridge shouted.

"Sighted," one of the marksmen answered.

"Get them," Boxer ordered.

The two rifles snapped simultaneously.

"One is gone," the officer on the bridge shouted.

The chief of the ERT keyed Boxer. "Skipper, there's nothing but bits and pieces of the raft here."

"Are you sure?" Boxer asked.

"Positive."

"Return to the *Shark*," Boxer said.

"Ten four," the chief answered.

Boxer walked back slowly and climbed up to the sail.

"ERT aboard," Cowly reported.

"Clear the deck," Boxer said. "Prepare to dive."

Cowly relayed Boxer's orders over the MC.

"Clear the bridge," Boxer said. "Cowly, you have the CONN. Have the DO make one thousand feet. We'll stay at that depth until we dive for the cave."

"Aye, aye, Skipper," Cowly answered.

Oblivious to the activity around him, Boxer left the bridge and went directly to his quarters. He dropped down on the chair and, resting his elbows on the desk, he buried his face in his hands.

Cowly keyed Boxer. "Skipper, Captain Borodine requests permission to speak with you."

"Have him escorted to my cabin," Boxer responded.

"Aye, aye, Skipper," Cowly said.

A few minutes later, Boxer answered a soft knock on his door with, "Come." He stood up.

The door opened and one of Vargas's men said, "Comrade Captain Borodine, Skipper."

"Thanks," Boxer told him. "I'll call the bridge when I need you."

"Aye, aye, Skipper," the man answered.

"Please come in," Boxer said.

Borodine entered the cabin and closed it behind him. He looked around and said, "Not much room here either."

Boxer nodded.

"I came to personally offer my sympathy to you," Borodine said. "It is one thing to lose men in action, but to have them killed while trying to save others is a different matter altogether."

Boxer gestured to the chair. "Please, sit down."

"Thank you," Borodine said.

"I'd offer you a cigarette," Boxer said, "but I smoke a pipe."

"Your men have been very generous with the cigarettes," Borodine answered, taking a pack out of his pocket.

"I have a bottle of vodka, if you'd care for a drink?"

Borodine nodded and lit a cigarette.

"Did you manage to see Galena when you were in Paris?" Boxer asked, pouring vodka into two plastic glasses.

Borodine shook his head. "Only from a distance. I was afraid to go any closer. There was always the possibility that your people or mine would misunderstand."

Boxer nodded.

"To the men who were killed," Borodine said, raising

his glass.

Boxer repeated what Borodine had said.

They touched glasses and drank.

"I also came here," Borodine said, "to tell you that I had no choice but to lead my men—"

"I would have done the same," Boxer told him. "Yes, I would have done the same."

"Thank you," Borodine said, draining his glass.

Boxer finished his vodka and said, "Have a bit more."

Borodine shook his head, "No thank you."

"Ordinarily," Boxer said, "I don't drink while I'm aboard. But for you," he said with a smile, "I made the exception to the rule."

"We make a great many exceptions to all sorts of rules for each other, don't we?"

"We sure as hell do!" Boxer exclaimed.

"Have you ever thought that the time might come when you would destroy me?"

Boxer hesitated.

"I know I have thought about having to destroy you," Borodine said filling the gap.

"So have I," Boxer admitted.

Borodine nodded.

Beginning to feel uncomfortable with the tone of the conversation, Boxer said, "It is never easy to think about it, much less discuss it . . . For now neither of us has to be concerned with that situation. We can be friends."

"We are friends," Borodine said with conviction.

"I think that's what drives your people and mine more than slightly bonkers."

"What's this bonkers?"

"Crazy."

Borodine nodded vigorously, "Bonkers, eh? I like that word"

"Stick around," Boxer said, "and you'll pick up a few more."

"I really can't go any place," Borodine answered with a laugh.

"I guess you can't," Boxer answered. "But then again neither can I."

The two men became quiet again; then Borodine asked, "Are you married, Comrade Captain?"

"Divorced."

Borodine nodded. "I will soon marry again. She is going to have a baby any day now."

"That's wonderful!" Boxer exclaimed. "What's her name?"

"Irena," Borodine answered. "I'd show you a picture of her, but the snapshots I had were aboard the *Sea Savage.*"

"I'll see if I can establish radio contact with Moscow to find out how she is." Boxer said.

Borodine exploded with laughter. "That will surely drive my people bonkers."

Boxer laughed too.

"What about you, do you have someone you want to marry?"

"I'm waiting for her to decide," Boxer said. "I have a photograph of her." He removed Trish's picture from his wallet and handed it to Borodine. "Her name is Patricia, but everyone calls her Trish."

"She's very beautiful . . . But haven't I seen her before?" Borodine asked. "In Paris?"

The DO keyed Boxer. "Skipper, we're coming to two thousand feet."

"Ten four," Boxer answered. "Hold her there."

"Aye, aye, Skipper," the DO answered.

"Excuse me," Boxer said to Borodine. "Duty first."

"Yes, always."

Boxer keyed Cowly. "Hold our present position."

"Aye, aye, Skipper," Cowly answered.

Boxer turned his attention back to Borodine. "Yes,

she's the former wife of Congressman McElroy."

Borodine raised his eyebrows. "Is he the man who investigated you?"

"Yes. I met Trish in Paris."

"You became lovers there?"

Boxer nodded.

"I hope you find happiness with her," Borodine said, handing Trish's photo back to Boxer.

"Yes, I hope I do," Boxer answered.

"The kind of life we lead," Borodine said, "doesn't make it easy for a woman to be a wife."

Boxer agreed.

"Well," Borodine said, getting to his feet, "I've taken much more of your time than I had intended." He offered Boxer his hand. "But I enjoyed every moment of it."

"So did I," Boxer said, shaking Borodine's hand. "So did I. As soon as we finish with the cave, I'll try to establish radio contact."

"Thank you," Borodine said. "Thank you very much, but I wouldn't want any of our ships to get a fix on your position. No, I'll wait until I'm aboard one of our vessels."

Boxer opened the door. "Escort Comrade Captain Borodine back to the mess area," he told the guard.

"Aye, aye, Skipper," the man answered.

Four

Boxer studied the picture on the UWIS. To his left was Borodine. On his right was Dr. Suslov.

Boxer had managed to get her cooperation by promising he would not turn in any member of either the *Sea Savage*'s crew, or its scientific staff. Since he had already told Borodine that he would release all of them, he was pleased that he had gotten more out of the bargain than Suslov. But that was his and Borodine's secret.

"Steady, as she goes," Boxer told Mahony.

"Aye, aye, Skipper," the man answered.

The *Shark*'s high intensity lights illuminated the underwater seascape. Huge boulders were everywhere. Some were half the size of the *Shark*.

"Water temperature rising," Cowly reported. "Up zero four degrees."

Boxer glanced questioningly at Suslov.

"A volcanic fissure," she said, leaning slightly closer to the UWIS screen.

The SO keyed Boxer. "Change in bottom configuration, Skipper . . . Bearing one four four degrees . . . Range eleven thousand yards."

"Roger that," Boxer answered.

"That could be what we're looking for," Suslov said.

Boxer keyed the DO. "Give me five zero feet."

"Up five zero feet," the DO answered.

"Mahony," Boxer said, "come to course one four four degrees."

The DO keyed Boxer. "Holding at one thousand eighty feet."

"Roger that," Boxer responded.

"Temperature dropping," Cowly reported. "Five five degrees."

"We've left the area of the fissure," Suslov explained.

Boxer didn't answer. Suslov's right breast pressed against his shoulder.

"What is that?" Borodine asked, as a snakelike creature, with a phosphorescent head and transparent body swam by.

"Is this being video taped?" Suslov asked.

"Yes," Boxer answered.

"Then one of the other members of the team might be able to identify it," Suslov said.

The SO keyed Boxer. "Target bearing two three degrees . . . Range eighteen thousand yards . . . Speed two zero knots."

"ID it."

"Aye, aye, Skipper," the SO answered.

"We are looking at very old formations—probably as old, if not older than the Canadian Shield," Suslov said.

"There's the rise, dead ahead!" Borodine exclaimed.

Out of the blackness a gray shadow began to emerge that with each passing moment became more defined.

"The cave should be under that hill," Suslov said.

"And you're sure there's an entrance?" Boxer asked, looking up at her.

She shook her head. "Only that there's a cave there," she answered.

Boxer keyed the EO. "One zero knots."

"Going to one zero knots," the EO responded.

"Those minisubs would come in handy now," Boxer commented aloud.

"To bad you saw fit to waste them," Suslov said sarcastically.

Boxer was about to answer that by wasting them, he managed to save her life and the lives of everyone else aboard the *Shark*. But she already knew that and had spoken only to irritate him. She did. But he was determined not to give her the satisfaction of showing it. He remained silent.

"Skipper," the SO said, "target is *Tecumseh*."

"Roger that," Boxer answered and relayed the information to Cowly.

"Did you know she was going to be here?" Cowly asked.

"No," Boxer answered.

"Are you going to contact her?"

Boxer hesitated for a moment before he shook his head. "No. I don't know why she's here, and she doesn't know I'm here. I don't want Langly to know where the hell the *Shark* is and if I contact the *Tecumseh*, Rugger will have to notify Langly."

"Your supply ship?" Borodine asked.

Boxer nodded and didn't offer any further explanations.

"Skipper," the SO said, keying Boxer again, "one of the *T*'s propeller shafts is bent, or something is wrong with her bearings."

"Explain," Boxer said.

"The overall sound meets the *T*'s signature, but now and then there's a slight variation that could be caused by a bent shaft or bad bearings."

"Ten four," Boxer said. He gave Cowly the information the SO had given him.

"Rugger probably knows," Cowly answered.

"Probably," Boxer answered and gave his attention to the UWIS.

The undersea hill was sharply defined. It resembled a

woman's breast. It was at least thirty feet high and four hundred feet in diameter.

"There," Suslov suddenly exclaimed, pointing off to the left on the screen. "There's the entrance!"

Boxer keyed the EO. "Zero five knots."

"Going to zero five knots," the EO answered.

The SO keyed Boxer. "The *T* is passing out of range."

"Ten four," Boxer answered; then he said, "Helmsman, come to course three three two degrees."

"Coming to course three three two degrees," Mahony responded.

Boxer keyed the DO. "Stand by at the diving planes."

"Standing by at the diving planes," the DO answered.

The cave's opening was wide enough to allow the *Shark* to enter with a good six feet clearance on each side.

Boxer keyed the DO. "Zero five on the bow and stern planes."

"Zero five degrees on the bow and stern planes," the DO answered.

On the UWIS the *Shark* angled toward the mouth of the cave.

Boxer keyed the DO. "Null all diving planes."

"All diving planes at null," the DO reported.

The *Shark* slid into the opening of the cave.

"Water temperature constant," Cowly reported.

"Roger that," Boxer answered.

A giant squid was suddenly illuminated by the *Shark*'s high intensity lights.

"That must be thirty feet long," Borodine said.

"At least," Boxer answered.

"Are you sure all of this is being taped, Captain?" Suslov asked, leaning closer to him.

"Yes," he answered.

"The cave is narrowing," Borodine said.

Boxer keyed the EO. "Stand by to stop all engines."

"Standing by," the EO answered.

The *Shark* eased through a natural tunnel and into a bowl shaped chamber.

Boxer left the COMCOMP and raised the periscope. "Holy Christ!" Boxer exclaimed.

"Is it the way I predicted it would be," Suslov asked. "An air bubble—"

Boxer returned to the COMCOMP. "Stop all engines," he told the EO.

"Stopping all engines," the EO said.

Boxer keyed the DO. "Up three zero feet," he said.

"Up three zero feet," the DO answered.

The *Shark* broke water.

Boxer switched on the TV cameras and scanned the cave. It was circular and more than a mile across. Its walls were almost smooth and the dome was fifty feet above the surface of the water.

"Six zero percent methane," Cowly said.

"Methane?" Suslov questioned.

Boxer glanced at Cowly.

"Methane with traces of ammonia," Cowly answered.

Suslov eased away from the screen. She looked at Borodine and spoke rapidly in Russian; then she said in English, "We're in the midst of what was probably once part of the earth's atmosphere when it was still cooling. Isn't there any way we can take samples?

Boxer shook his head. "Not at this depth."

"The analysis of such samples could tell us so much about the atmosphere's past."

"I'm sorry," Boxer said. "I'm genuinely sorry."

"Then why did you come here," Suslov asked angrily. "Why?"

Boxer pursed his lips. He looked at Borodine and said, "You know why I came here, don't you?"

Borodine nodded.

"Then tell me, Comrade Captain Borodine," Suslov shouted. "Tell me!"

41

"To see if it really could be used for a base and if it could, destroy it," Borodine said.

"Destroy it!" Suslov shrieked.

"Neither your country nor mine will be able to use it," Boxer said.

"But what about its geological value?"

Boxer shook his head. "I'm sorry."

"Sorry! You're sorry," Suslov cried, hurling herself at Boxer and pummeling him with her fists.

Grabbing hold of her flailing arms, Borodine pulled her away. "I apologize for her," he said to Boxer.

"Don't you dare apologize for me!" Suslov shouted.

Borodine barked out something in Russian.

"You wouldn't dare have me put under arrest," she challenged.

He pointed to Boxer. "He will and should if you can't control yourself."

Boxer looked at the two of them. Satisfied that Borodine had quieted Suslov, he keyed the DO. "Take her down three zero feet."

"Down three zero feet," the DO answered.

The *Shark* got underway and turned back toward the narrow channel through which she had come.

"A find of a lifetime," Suslov said, "and you're going to destroy it."

Boxer didn't answer. He keyed the DO. "Take her up two five zero feet."

"Going up two five zero feet," the DO answered.

Boxer glanced at Suslov. She was taut with fury. He knew she was right. But he also knew that if he left it intact, either the Russians or his own people would try to use it.

"I will never forgive you," Suslov said to Borodine. "Never! If you hadn't told him about the cave, none of this would be happening."

"He is doing what I would do in his place," Borodine said.

42

"Traitor," she hissed. "Capitalistic traitor!"

Boxer turned toward her. "Stop it!" he ordered. "Stop the nonsense. Comrade Captain Borodine is not a traitor and you know it. You also know that the cave must be destroyed."

Suslov clenched her teeth and looked away.

"We're exiting the cave," Boxer reported. He keyed the aft torpedo officer. "Load tubes five and six."

"Aye, aye, Skipper," the TO answered.

Boxer switched on the Autofire Control equipment and set it for two thousand yards.

The TO keyed Boxer. "Torpedos ready in tubes five and six."

"Arm torpedos five and six," Boxer said.

"Torpedos five and six armed."

"Fire control on automatic," Boxer said.

The TO repeated what Boxer said.

Boxer watched the instruments on the Autofire Control section of the COMCOMP. "Three zero seconds and counting," he said, looking at Borodine and then at Suslov.

Suslov shook her head.

"One five seconds," Boxer said.

Suslov gasped and began to whimper.

"Mark," Boxer said.

There was the sound of escaping air. The stern of the *Shark* rose slightly and then settled down.

Boxer watched the Distance to Target Clock. Ninety seconds equaled the two thousand yards. The instant a red light began to flash the thunderous sound of an enormous explosion rolled over the *Shark*. Within moments a powerful shockwave thrust the *Shark* up another fifty feet.

"The two torpedos must have struck at the same time or within a few seconds of each other," Boxer commented, as the *Shark* began to sink to her former depth.

43

Borodine agreed.

"Helmsman, come to course three three two degrees," Boxer said.

"Coming to course three three two degrees," Mahony answered.

The *Shark* returned to where the cave had been.

Suslov moved closer to Boxer and looket at the UWIS. "The top of the hill is gone," she said in a whisper.

"The sea has it now," Borodine commented.

Boxer nodded and keyed the DO. "Make five hundred feet."

"Going to five hundred feet," the DO answered.

Boxer switched on the MC. "Now hear this . . . Now hear this . . . This is the captain speaking . . . The *Shark* will be returning to her home base . . . The *Shark* will be returning to her home base . . . But first we will find safe transportation home for our guests." He turned to Borodine and smiled. "Your choice, Comrade Captain Borodine. What will it be—warship, freighter or fishing vessel?"

"Whatever luck brings our way," Borodine answered.

Boxer smiled. He knew it wouldn't have anything to do with luck. With a touch of a few keys he'd have the disposition of every Russian ship in the Pacific and choose the closest one. But that could wait. Now he wanted to relax for awhile.

"Skipper," the COMMO said, "there's heavy traffic between this fishing trawler and Moscow."

Boxer smiled. "Roger that," he said and repeated the message to Borodine, who was standing alongside of him on the deck of the *Shark*. The two of them had emerged from the sail as soon as the *Shark* had heaved to within a few yards of the trawler's starboard side. "Better tell the captain what's in store for him," Boxer said, pressing the

MC key on the portable radio and handing it to Borodine.

Borodine nodded. He spoke in Russian, identified himself and told the captain that he, his crew and four scientists would be coming aboard the *Boris Tsindelis*.

The captain looked down at them from the bridge, and using a bull horn, he answered.

"He says," Borodine translated, "that he is waiting word from Moscow."

"Tell him that I don't have that luxury," Boxer said. "Tell him either he takes all of you aboard, or I dump you in the ocean."

Borodine did a double take, smiled and translated Boxer's words; then to Boxer he said, "He'll radio that to Moscow."

Boxer nodded and wondered how one of our trawler captains would act in a similar situation?

The captain spoke again.

"He'll take us aboard," Borodine said, handing the radio back to him.

"Cowly," Boxer said, "stand by to have our guests come on deck."

"Ten four," Cowly answered from the sail's bridge.

"The crew will go first; then the officers and finally you, your EXO and the four civilians," Boxer said.

Borodine nodded.

Suddenly the captain spoke again.

Borodine went pale. He almost staggered.

"What's wrong?" Boxer asked.

"Irena and the baby—" he turned away.

"What about them?"

"Both dead," Borodine said, stifling a sob.

Boxer put his hand on Borodine's shoulder. There was nothing he could say that would be meaningful.

After a few moments, Borodine said, "I'm all right." He wiped the tears from his eyes, blew his nose and faced Boxer.

"How did it happen?"

Borodine shook his head. "I'll be told later."

The first three crew men came on deck. They saluted Boxer and Borodine.

They returned the salutes.

Two boats were lowered from the trawler and in a matter of minutes all of the enlisted men were taken off the *Shark*.

Boxer shook hands with Viktor and whispered, "Your captain has had bad news from home. Look after him."

Viktor nodded, released Boxer's hand and stepped into the boat. With the exception of Borodine and the scientists, all of the Russians had cleared the *Shark*.

"Well," Borodine said, "it's time to say good-by." He held out his hand to Boxer.

"No handshake, Igor," Boxer told him and he embraced him.

"Thank you for saving us," Borodine said.

"Perhaps we will meet again in Paris," Boxer responded.

"Maybe," Borodine answered, stepping away and leaping into the waiting boat.

Suslov stopped in front of Boxer and looked straight at him. "I hate everything you stand for," she said. "I can never forgive you for blowing up the cave and—"

"Shut up," Boxer said.

"What did you say?"

Boxer swept Suslov into his arms and kissed her hard on her lips. Then he opened his mouth.

She did the same.

The men from both ships cheered.

"It's damn hard to kiss someone when they're talking," Boxer said.

Suslov was too surprised to speak.

"You're much too beautiful a woman to go around hating," Boxer said with a smile.

"That was not supposed to happen," she whispered.

Boxer smiled and helped her into the boat.

Doctors Gregory Chekurov, Valdimir Travkin and Alexandar Kassov stepped in front of Boxer and shook his hand before they stepped into the boat.

Borodine signaled the coxswain to ease the boat away from the *Shark*.

Boxer keyed Cowly. "Stand by to get underway."

"Aye, aye, Skipper," Cowly answered.

Boxer watched the boat slide toward the trawler. He looked up. The sky was a lovely blue, and on the horizon several huge cumulus clouds looked like castles. He looked back at the boat and waved.

Borodine and Suslov waved back.

Suddenly Dr. Kassov stood up and shouted, "I'm not going back. I'm not going back!" Before anyone could stop him, he was in the water and swimming with powerful strokes toward the *Shark*.

Boxer hit the remote MC. "Switch . . . Emergency . . . Emergency on deck . . Rifle squad topside on the double . . . Machine gunners man your weapons . . . Stand by . . . Cowly sound general quarters."

Instantly the klaxon began to blow.

Boxer watched Kassov. He was a short, fat man with thinning hair and a pock marked face. Boxer couldn't remember what his specialty was.

Borodine ordered the oarsmen to backwater.

"Ship oars," Boxer called out.

There was less than ten yards between Kassov and the *Shark*.

"That's close enough!" Boxer warned.

"Ship oars," Borodine shouted.

The captain of the *Boris Tsindelis* blew the ship's whistle three times and men rushed to the side with automatic weapons.

"Come back to the boat," Borodine urged. "I promise you no harm will come to you."

Kassov continued to swim toward the *Shark*.

There was a sharp exchange between Borodine and the trawler's captain. Then Borodine shouted something in Russian to Kassov.

Boxer switched on the MC. "Comrade Captain Borodine," Boxer said, "tell the men aboard the trawler to put up the weapons. Tell them that if they don't put up their weapons, I will order my machine gunner to open fire."

Borodine looked at Boxer, then relayed the order to the men.

The captain of the *Tsindelis* shouted at Borodine.

But Borodine shouted back.

Kassov finally reached the *Shark*. Two men from the gun crew pulled him aboard.

"Take him below," Boxer said; then over the MC, he said, "It's over Comrade Captain Borodine. Doctor Kassov is aboard."

Borodine signaled the men to begin to row again.

"Stand by to dive," Boxer said over the MC. "All hands clear the deck . . . All hands clear the deck . . . Clear the deck!"

Five

The *Shark* headed for her berth. Boxer and Cowly were on the sail's bridge.

"Three cars and three people," Cowly said.

"That sporty looking job belongs to Trish," Boxer explained.

"She must be the one waving." Cowly said.

"You can bet it's not Kinkade and admirals don't wave," Boxer responded, training his binoculars on Trish. She wore a light blue skirt and a white blouse. Though it was only June, she had a good tan and she had let her blond hair grow down to her shoulders.

A fourth car pulled up.

"That one is for Kassov," Boxer said, lowering his glasses.

"He's going to be debriefed."

"Have you spoken to him?" Cowly asked.

"Tried . . . But he's not the talkative type."

"Do you think he regrets defecting?"

Boxer shrugged, but didn't say anything. He gave his full attention now to the movement of the *Shark*. "Steady as she goes," he said.

"Steady as she goes," Mahony echoed.

Boxer nodded and keyed the EO. "Stop all engines."

"All engines stopped," the EO answered.

Boxer switched on the MC. "Stand by on the bow

lines." He waited until the *Shark* drifted alongside of the pier. "Let go bow lines." He checked the stern. "Let go stern lines . . . Secure all lines."

"All lines secured," the deck chief responded on a bullhorn.

"Roger that," Boxer said over the MC. He looked at Cowly smiled and then said, "Now hear this . . . Now hear this . . . This is the captain speaking . . . Secure all systems . . . Secure all systems . . . Liberty commences at fourteen hundred."

"Doctor Kassov," Boxer called, coming out on to the *Shark*'s deck from the sail.

Kassov and the two Company men with him stopped and turned.

"I wasn't going to let you go without saying goodby," Boxer said.

Kassov managed a slight smile. "It was kind of you to come."

Boxer shook his hand. "Good luck and good health, doctor," he said.

Kassov nodded. "Thank you for everything."

"You'll be fine," Boxer told him.

"Yes, I'm sure I will," he said. "But I am very anxious about the future. I feel as if I'm skating on very thin ice and I'm in danger of falling through . . . Do you know the feeling, Captain?"

"Yes, I know the feeling," Boxer answered. "But you will be fine."

"Yes, I am sure I will," Kassov said. "I am sure I will." Then he nodded to the men with him, turned, crossed the gangplank and headed for the Company limo.

Boxer watched him for a few moments and for the first time realized that Kassov was a very courageous man.

"Well, are you just going to stand there?" Trish called,

running toward him.

Boxer cleared the *Shark*.

"I missed you!" she exclaimed, throwing herself into his arms.

"I missed you too," he said and pressed her tightly to him.

"Your grandfather and the admiral are coming toward us," he said.

"That's a hell of a thing to tell me now," she chided.

He kissed the tip of her nose. "I can't salute the admiral, or shake hands with your grandfather with you in my arms."

"Which would you rather do?"

"Shake hands with you and kiss the admiral," Boxer answered.

Trish laughed and stepped away.

Boxer saluted Stark.

"Good to see you back," Stark said, returning the salute.

"Good to be back," Boxer responded.

Stark extended his hand and Boxer shook it.

Boxer extended his hand to Kinkade.

"At least you managed to bring one Ruskie back," Kinkade commented dryly.

"I didn't bring him back," Boxer said. "He came of his own free will."

Kinkade nodded. "I'll see the two of you for dinner, won't I, Trish?"

"Yes," Trish answered.

"Seven o'clock at the Oak Room," Kinkade said. He turned to Stark. "Will you be there too?"

"I'd like it if you were there," Trish said, looking at Stark.

He nodded and said, "Then I'll be there."

Kinkade and Stark returned to their limos and in a matter of minutes were gone.

"Well, sailor, are you free?" Trish asked.

"More or less," Boxer said, "I have a few things to take care of and then I'll pick up my gear and we can go."

Suddenly the MC came on. "Now hear this . . . Now hear this . . . Liberty has commenced . . . All personnel must sign off . . . All personnel must leave an active phone number where they can be contacted, or must make provisions to phone our central number a minimum of three times every twenty four hours."

The first few men on liberty emerged from the sail, saluted the flag and then hurried ashore.

"See you, Skipper," one of them said.

Boxer nodded.

"Take care, Skipper," another one said.

"You too," Boxer answered.

Each man that passed him said something.

And Boxer always answered.

"Don't they have to salute you?" Trish asked.

"There's no saluting aboard the *Shark*," Boxer said.

"Then why did you salute the admiral?"

Boxer laughed. "He's not a member of the crew and he is an admiral."

They started to walk back to the gangplank.

"You wait in the car," Boxer said. "I'll only be a few minutes."

"I want to go on board with you . . . Can't I? Please. I've never been on a submarine before."

"Never?"

Trish shook her head, making her long blond hair swirl from side to side.

"Okay," Boxer said. "I'll even give you a tour." He took hold of her hand and led her over the gangplank on to the deck.

Vargas emerged from the sail. "Hey Skipper, she's beautiful."

Boxer kissed the back of Trish's hand. "She's mine

Spic. You have your own lady."

Vargas grinned.

Boxer introduced Trish to Vargas and said, "Spic, how about you and your Russian lady joining us for dinner some night."

"Sure, Skipper. You just give me a call a day before."

"Will do," Boxer said.

"She's too beautiful for you," Vargas said with a grin and hurried off the *Shark*.

"He's quite a character, isn't he?" Trish asked.

"I guess he is. But he's a good officer and a good friend," Boxer said.

"He's crazy about you," Trish said. "But not as crazy as I am."

"I hope not," he said, leading her into the sail. "And I hope not in the same way."

"Him . . . Never . . . He's a macho man if there ever was one," she answered.

"That's the way he comes across," Boxer said, "but he really is a very gentle person."

"Where are we now?" Trish asked, looking around her.

"In the sail, which is only raised when we're on the surface."

"And where are we going?" she questioned.

"To the bridge," Boxer answered. "That's where I spend most of my time."

Cowly was still there.

Boxer introduced Trish to Cowly; then he asked, "Why haven't you gone?"

"A few things to be done, Skipper," Cowly answered.

"I have a few to do myself," Boxer said.

The two men shook hands.

Boxer took Trish on a complete tour of the *Shark* and explained as much as he could without breaching security.

"I'm impressed," she told him. "I'm impressed that you run the whole show."

"I don't run it," Boxer said. "I only oversee it and make certain decisions about what to do and how to do it."

"You run it," she said. "Even granddad knows that."

They finally wound up in his quarters.

"I wondered what this place looked like," she said. "It's smaller than I had imagined."

"That's what the Russian doctor said too," he answered, as he went through the shut down procedures for the COMCOMP.

"What doctor?"

"Louise Suslov, a geologist and a full colonel in the KGB," he answered, without looking at Trish.

"Another woman was in this room?" she asked.

Boxer chuckled.

"What's so funny?"

"I surprised the hell out of her. She came up on deck to board the long boat that was going to take her to the Russian trawler. She told me how much she hated me and the capitalistic system. Before she could finish I told her to shut up. She did and I took her in my arms and kissed the hell out of her."

"Open mouthed?"

"If I had," he lied, "she would have gone into cardiac arrest . . . No, just one long, hard kiss on the lips was enough to take her breath away."

"And here I was feeling sorry for you and refusing the opportunities that came my way."

"What opportunities?" Boxer asked absently.

"Sexual opportunities, of course," Trish said.

"Sexual opportunities," Boxer repeated, turning toward her. "What are you talking about?"

"I never let a man near me when you were away," she said. "And you tell me about the way you kissed some

54

Russian vamp."

"You have to be joking!" Boxer exclaimed, as he stood up. "Com'on Trish."

Cowly keyed him. "Skipper, word just came in that the *T* is due tomorrow at fourteen hundred hours. She's running into heavy weather off Hatteras."

"Ten four," Boxer answered; then asked, "Any word on where she has been?"

"Negative."

"Ten four," Boxer answered.

"Can you be called any time like that?" Trish asked.

Boxer nodded. "When I'm on board, yes. Twenty four hours a day . . . Seven days a week."

Trish shook her head. "I had no idea."

Boxer smiled. "How could you? Listen, I have a few more minutes' work; then we can get out of here."

She nodded.

Boxer keyed Cowly. "Try to raise the *T* on our own radio . . . I want to speak to Rugger about that shaft or bad bearing the *T* has."

"Aye, aye, Skipper," Cowly answered.

"What's going on?" Trish asked.

Rather than explain, Boxer said, "Just ship talk between captains."

Trish lit a cigarette.

Cowly keyed Boxer. "Skipper, I can't raise the *T*. I checked with HQ and they can't raise her either. The storm is a bad one. Everything in its vicinity is having trouble."

"Thanks for trying," Boxer said.

"Ten four, Skipper," Cowly answered.

"You'll meet Rugger in a few days."

"Rugger?"

"The captain of the *T*—I mean the *Tecumseh*. He's a very good friend of mine."

"I'm finished," Boxer said, striking several keys sequentially on the MINICOMCOMP. He stood up and turned toward Trish.

She stubbed out her cigarette and said, "Let's do it now."

Her eyes moved to the bunk. "There's just enough room."

Unbuttoning her blouse, she came toward him.

Boxer grinned. "You are something else!" he said, taking her into his arms and kissing her lips; then on the neck.

She circled his neck with her arms and pressed herself against him. "You're hard," she said.

"You wouldn't want me soft, would you?"

"God no!"

Boxer undid the remaining button of her blouse, eased it off and dropped it on the chair. Her bra was white, made of very thin material and cupped on the bottom part of the breasts, leaving the tops exposed. Boxer ran his fingers over one and then the other. They were warm and soft. He reached around Trish and undid the back of the bra.

"Kiss them," she whispered.

He took one erect nipple into his mouth and sucked at it.

"I like that so much," she said.

Boxer did the same to the other nipple.

"Harder," Trish said, pressing her hands on the back of his head. "Oh do it harder!"

Boxer scored the nipple between his teeth.

"Yes . . . Yes . . . That's it!" she gasped.

Boxer was intoxicated with the smell of her, with the feel of her warm flesh against his face. He let go of her nipple and kissed her midriff. Then he undid the button in the back of the skirt and pulled the zipper down.

Of its own weight, the skirt slowly slid down to the floor.

With her right foot, Trish eased the skirt to the side.

Boxer pushed her briefs down. Like her bra they were made of thin white material. He put his hand over the dark honey colored tuft of her love mound.

Trish undressed Boxer and when he was as naked as she, she pressed herself against him. "I don't know which is worse," she said, "to have a hard-on, or feel an emptiness that must be filled."

"We'll discuss it later," Boxer said, running his hands over her buns and squeezing them.

"God, I love you!" Trish said, caressing his organ.

"And I love you," he told her.

Open mouth they kissed.

Boxer lifted Trish into his arms and gently set her down on the bunk.

"It has your scent," she said, raising her arms to him. "Come inside of me now . . . Oh how I want you there!"

Boxer started to enter her.

Trish raised her hips to make it easier for him. "That feels marvelous," she said.

Boxer buried his face in the curve of her neck and inhaled the scent of her rose perfume. "I'll never again be able to sleep here without thinking about this," he told her.

"That's what happens to me when I'm alone in my bed," she said. "I think of the things we did in it . . . The pleasure we gave each other."

Boxer began to move.

Trish closed her eyes. "Finger me," she whispered. "Finger me, my darling."

Boxer moved one hand under her buttock and teased her bunhole.

Trish caressed his scrotum.

"I could be courtmartialed for this," Boxer said.

"This is a hell of a time to mention it to me."

"I just thought you'd like to know the risk I'm willing

57

to take for you."

"And I'd willingly die for you, Jack . . . I mean it . . . I really do."

Boxer put his lips gently on hers.

She put her arms around his neck. "You fill me exquisitely," she said.

"You hold me exquisitely," he answered.

Trish closed her eyes.

Boxer kissed each lid. He wanted to ask her to marry him. But before he left he had agreed to wait until she told him that she was ready to marry again.

"When you were away," she said, "I thought about all the sexy things we'd do when you came back. But now all I want is to be fucked by you . . . Just a simple, good screwing."

"Are you getting what you want?"

"Oh yes, my darling. Are you getting what you want?"

"Absolutely," Boxer answered.

Trish arched her body, pushing her hips against him. He drove down.

"God, that feels so wonderful!" Trish exclaimed.

Boxer quickened his thrusts.

"Yes . . . Yes . . . Do it faster . . . Harder!" she cried out, wrapping her naked legs around his back.

Boxer kissed her lips.

Trish gave him her tongue.

"I love you," Boxer said, lifting his mouth from hers.

"Oh Jack . . . Oh Jack!" she exclaimed.

Boxer could feel her body tense.

"I'm coming . . . I'm coming," Trish cried, smashing her hips into Boxer.

He thrust his body down and the next instant whirled into the ecstasy of his own climax, where an explosion of colors filled his brain and he could hear himself growl with pleasure.

"Oh my God!" Trish exclaimed, pointing to the door.

Boxer looked over his shoulder and saw Cowly standing in the open doorway. He was very pale. His hands were shaking. There was a noticeable tic just below his right eye and an expression of complete disgust on his face.

Cowly licked his lips. "You didn't answer the key," he explained.

"For godsakes get him out of here!" Trish screamed.

"What the hell—" Boxer started to say.

"The *T*—" Cowly hesitated.

"Are you going to get him out of here?" Trish cried.

"What about the *T*?" Boxer asked.

"She's breaking up."

"What?" Boxer almost leaped up, but he remembered that he was Trish's only cover. "Stand by on the bridge . . . I'll be there in a few minutes."

"Aye, aye, Skipper," Cowly answered, stepping back and closing the door.

"He was there watching us!" Trish exclaimed.

Boxer eased himself off of her nude body.

"He's a creep . . . A real sicky!" Trish said.

"We'll talk about it later," Boxer said, putting on his shorts and trousers. "I have to go to the bridge now."

Trish pushed herself up on her elbows. "He probably was there all the time," she said.

Boxer shrugged.

"Aren't you going to do anything about it?" she asked.

"There's nothing I can do," Boxer said. "We . . . I was the one who was doing something wrong."

"Can't you transfer him off the *Shark*?"

Boxer shook his head. "He's an excellent EXO . . . He did nothing wrong."

"He stood there like some fucking queer and watched us screw," Trish said angrily.

"I have to go to the bridge," Boxer said. "Get dressed. The bathroom is through that door there."

Trish pouted.

Boxer bent down and kissed her on the forehead; then he left his cabin and went to the bridge.

When Boxer reached the bridge, Cowly was busy at the COMMO section of the COMCOMP.

"Nothing else has been sent," he said.

Boxer nodded. He could see that Cowly was still tense enough for the tic to be visible. He contacted Central Naval Communications Center and asked for word on the *Tecumseh*.

"Last we heard was that she was breaking up," the officer said. "We have a rescue ship on the way and planes are standing by to go to the scene as soon as the weather clears."

"Ten four," Boxer answered.

Suddenly the radio phone rang.

Boxer picked up and identified himself.

"This is Kinkade," the voice said. "I have Stark patched in. The *Tecumseh* is breaking up off Hatteras."

"Jack, this is Stark . . . Be in my office in an hour."

"Admiral, I want to go out there. I can still contact Vargas and a few of the other men. We know what to do. Maybe I can get enough of a crew together to use the *Shark*."

"We'll talk about it," Kinkade said.

"There's no time to talk about it," Boxer said. "Admiral, the *Shark* can be there in a matter of hours . . . Even if the weather is bad, we can search."

"He's got a point there," Stark said.

"The *Shark* needs repairs," Kinkade said.

"She's in good enough shape to do this," Boxer responded.

"The Coast Guard is on its way," said Kinkade.

"Admiral, Rugger is a good friend of mine," Boxer said.

"Alright, see how much of the crew you can put together. Anything less than fifty percent and you stay in port."

"Roger that," Boxer said.

"Keep in close contact," Stark said. "I want to know exactly what's happening . . . You have two days; then I want you back in port."

"Yes, sir," Boxer answered. He put the phone down.

"I'll go," Cowly said.

"I didn't think you wouldn't," Boxer answered; then he said, "Get as many men back as you can. I need operating personnel, but I'll take whatever we get. Contact Vargas . . . I need a dozen good divers."

"Aye, aye, Skipper," Cowly said and he turned to go.

"Just a minute Bob," Boxer said, "I want to talk to you."

Cowly faced him.

"What happened, happened. There was no way you could know what I was doing."

"I did key you," Cowly said.

Boxer nodded. "I didn't hear you. It's not a disaster."

Cowly shook his head. "I guess it isn't."

"Okay, you get moving on bringing the men back," Boxer said, "and I'll see Trish off the *Shark*. I want to put to sea within two hours if possible; three at the very most."

"Aye, aye, Skipper," Cowly said.

Boxer nodded and returned to his cabin.

Dressed, Trish sat at the desk. "Now will you tell me why that man had to—"

"The *Tecumseh* is breaking up off Hatteras," Boxer said.

"What's the *Tecumseh*?" she asked, lighting a ciga-

61

rette and puffing on it violently.

"The *Shark*'s mother ship," Boxer explained. "Listen, Trish, I can't go with you. The *Shark* is going to sea again in a couple of hours."

"For how long?"

"Two, maybe three days. We're going to look for survivors."

"Good God, you just came in!"

"Trish, I volunteered to go. Rugger would do no less if the *Shark* was in trouble."

"Then there's nothing for me to say," she said, getting to her feet.

"I'll take you to your car."

"You sure that won't interfere with your rescue mission?" she asked sarcastically.

"That kind of remark is beneath you," Boxer said.

"I'm sorry. But I was hoping to have you to myself for a while."

Boxer pursed his lips. "I'll be back in two or three days."

Trish nodded.

Boxer opened the door; then closed it. He grabbed hold of Trish and spun her into his arms. "I owe it to those men," he said.

"And what do you owe me?" she asked. "Don't answer now. Think about it. We just finished making love. Think about what you owe me, Jack."

He moved to kiss her.

"No . . . I don't feel like it," Trish said.

Boxer let go of her, opened the door and escorted her up on deck.

"You don't have to come down to the car with me," Trish said.

Boxer nodded. "Will I see you when I return?" he asked.

Trish nodded. "I can't stop myself from loving you;

nor can I stop myself from being angry."

"Don't be angry," Boxer said gently. "I know this isn't easy for you to understand. In your place I wouldn't understand it either, but—"

"No explanations please," she said, holding up her hand. "I'll see you when you return. I'll be on the pier waiting."

Boxer hugged her fiercely; then he let her go.

Trish turned and hurried down the gangplank.

Six

Less than an hour at sea and the *Shark* began to feel the effects of the storm. The sky was lead gray. Minute by minute the wind became stronger until it screamed and turned the ordinary two to three foot waves into monsters of twenty or more feet. The *Shark* pitched, rolled and yawed as she fought her way south.

"Barometer is down another tenth," Cowly said.

He and Boxer were on the sail's bridge.

"The rain will start soon," Boxer said, "and we'll lose what visibility we have."

"And there's not much of that," Cowly answered. "And not much daylight left either. According to the almanac, about two hours, and given the weather, I'd say we'll be losing what light we have in considerably less time than that."

Boxer nodded. "Have COMMO send out a general signal to all shipping that we're in the vicinity of three four and three seven north latitude and seven four and seven eight east longitude."

Cowly immediately transmitted the coordinates to the Communications Officer.

"We'll dive as soon as it begins to rain, or we lose the light, whichever comes first."

Cowly didn't answer.

The Radar Officer keyed Boxer. "Beginning to pick up

several surface targets."

"Roger that," Boxer answered. "Report those that come within five zero zero yards."

"Aye, aye, Skipper," the RO said.

"I wrote to Admiral Stark requesting a different assignment," Cowly said above the howling wind.

Boxer looked at him.

"It will be the best thing all the way around," Cowly said.

"He won't be able to give you another assignment . . . It's the *Shark* or—"

"Then I'll take the resignation," Cowly said.

"That's crazy. I haven't asked you to go and I don't want you to. You're an excellent EXO. No, you're good enough to command your own boat."

Cowly shook his head.

"I've forgotten about the incident," Boxer said. "Besides, I was the one at fault."

"Mrs. McElroy was right," Cowly said, "I stood there and watched . . . I was there—"

"I probably would have too, had I been you."

For a few moments Cowly remained silent, then he said, "There's more to it . . . Much more."

"Okay, you're in love with Trish," Boxer responded, saying the first thing that came into his mind.

"No . . . I have never been in love with a woman."

Boxer's heart skipped a beat and began to race. He didn't look at Cowly, but he wanted to.

"But I have been in love with men," Cowly said.

Boxer pursed his lips. He wasn't quite sure what his reaction should be.

"Now do you understand?" Cowly asked.

"I can't give you an answer now," Boxer said. "I have to think about what I understand, or don't understand . . . But your sexual preferences have had nothing to do with your performance aboard the *Shark* . . . And that's the bottom line to me . . . That and—"

"I have never touched a man aboard, or given any man reason to believe that I'm anything but an all-around stud."

"I didn't think you had," Boxer answered.

"I'm glad you know," Cowly said. "I'm sorry it had to come as an aftermath to—"

"I already told you, I was to blame for it happening . . . not you!"

Cowly said nothing.

The COMMO keyed Boxer. "Skipper, Admiral Stark is on the radio."

"Patch him through," Boxer said.

"Aye, aye, Skipper," the COMMO responded.

"Can you hear me?" Stark asked.

"Yes," Boxer said.

"What kind of crew do you have?"

"All operating officers and better than eight zero percent of my operating crew."

"Repeat, please."

Boxer stated the numbers again.

"Very good," Stark said.

"Vargas and six divers are aboard."

"That's very good," Stark commented; then he said, "I listened to your tape. The *Tecumseh* had a bent starboard shaft. She was on her way back from a mission when you picked her up. The two of you came back on the same course. She was about ten hours behind you. You lost time when you went into the cave; then when you went looking for a ship to put Borodine and his crew aboard."

"Thanks for the fill in," Boxer said.

"What's the weather like?"

"Not good."

"Sounds terrible," Stark said.

"It's worse."

66

"Good luck, Jack," Stark said.

"I'm going to need it—and Rugger is going to need more," Boxer answered.

"Ten four," Stark said.

Boxer put the phone down and turning to Cowly, he said, "If he wasn't damn worried, Stark wouldn't have called."

"He has something to worry about. The barometer is down another tenth."

Boxer checked it. "The last time I saw it so low, we were coming out of the Arctic."

Cowly nodded.

"About that letter you were going to send," Boxer said, "I can't stop you from sending it, but I am not asking you to. And to put your sexual preferences in perspective, I don't care if you fuck rabbits, as long as you don't fuck them aboard the *Shark*."

Cowly hesitated; then he said, "I won't send it. But if you should ever change your mind—"

"Let's drop it. We have more important things to do now than worry about whether or not I'll change my mind at some future date."

"It's dropped," Cowly answered.

The RO keyed Boxer. "Heavy rain five thousand yards ahead."

"Can we go around it easily?"

"It goes off the scope from east to west," the RO said.

"Roger that," Boxer answered and he switched on the MC. "Clear the bridge . . . All hands clear the bridge . . . Prepare to dive . . . Prepare to dive." He hit the klaxon three times.

Within moments the outside bridge detail was inside the sail. Boxer and Cowly were on the bridge. Boxer was seated at the COMCOMP and Cowly was at his station.

Boxer keyed the DO. "Dive control on manual . . . Make one zero zero feet."

"Making one zero zero feet," the DO answered.

The hiss of air filled the *Shark* as water poured into the ballast tanks and the *Shark* began to slide beneath the wind-tortured surface.

"Lower sail," Boxer said to Cowly.

"Lowering sail," Cowly answered.

Boxer keyed the EO. "Reduce speed to one five knots."

"Going to one five knots," the EO answered.

Boxer watched the DDROT and now and then checked the depth gauge above the COMCOMP. Both were in synch.

The DO keyed Boxer. "Coming to one zero zero feet, Skipper."

"Roger that," Boxer answered. He watched the Electronic Level Indicator go to a null position.

"Dive completed." the DO reported.

"Roger that," Boxer answered. He stood up, removed his foul weather gear and placed it on its hook.

At a depth of a hundred feet, the *Shark* held a steady course without any of the pitching, rolling or yawing she experienced on the surface.

The COMMO keyed Boxer. "Skipper, the CG cutter *Trade Wind* picked up our last message and wants our position."

Boxer frowned. "Negative," he answered.

"Will transmit . . . Ten four."

Boxer switched on the UWIS, the high intensity lights and the Sonar Screen. "The bottom is another one zero five feet below us," he commented to Cowly.

The COMMO keyed Boxer again. "The *Trade Wind*'s captain has asked for our position again. He says he doesn't want to pick us up on his sonar and then go through the IDing procedure, when he has more important things to do."

"Ask for his position," Boxer said. "Tell him that we'll

keep track of him."

"Ten four, Skipper," the COMMO answered.

"Skipper," Cowly said, "we're within a few miles of the Gulf Stream. It's just possible that the *T* broke up in the stream and the wreckage is being carried north by it."

"We'll check it out in a few hours," Boxer said.

For a third time, the COMMO keyed Boxer. "Skipper, I sent your message, but the *Trade Wind* doesn't answer."

"Probably the weather is screwing up communications," Boxer said.

"You want me to keep trying?"

"Negative. If they make contact with you again, repeat my message."

"Ten four," the COMMO answered.

During the next three days, Boxer searched several hundred square miles of ocean. There was no sign of the *Tecumseh*, or her crew. No wreckage and no survivors.

Some of the time he thought about Trish. Any woman would have been upset by what had happened; he understood that. What he didn't understand was her selfishness. He was beginning to wonder if they could ever make a life together. He could have her pulling on him to give more of himself to her and less to the Company. He didn't want to go through again what he had gone through with his ex-wife, Gwen.

By the end of the third day the storm had blown itself out and the *Shark* surfaced into a late afternoon of white billowy clouds and columns of golden sunlight.

Boxer was back on the bridge. Despite the reason for him being there, he couldn't help but respond to the beauty of the sea and the sky. The beams of sunlight looked as if they were supporting the clouds.

Cowly joined him. "Are we going to continue the search?" he asked.

Boxer uttered a deep sigh. "Not much point to it,

is there?"

"No," Cowly answered.

Boxer keyed the COMMO. "Send a message to Stark and Kinkade that we're abandoning the search and will return to Norfolk. Our ETA should be twenty two hundred tonight."

"Ten four," the COMMO answered.

"Luckily there isn't any Mrs. Rugger," Boxer commented.

"I'd have to agree with that . . . but a good number of men aboard the *T* had wives."

"I wouldn't want to have to explain what happened to them."

"Who will explain?"

"Williams. His company owns the *T*," Boxer explained. "Even if it's a CIA operation, Williams is the person who will do the explaining."

Cowly shook his head. "I wouldn't want to be in his shoes."

"Nor would I," Boxer answered.

The COMMO keyed Boxer. "Skipper, I picked up a coded transmission."

"Ruskie?"

"No. It doesn't decode."

"Could it be a new code?"

"It might be," the COMMO answered.

"Isolate it and we'll turn it over to the Cryptosection."

"Aye, aye, Skipper," the COMMO said.

"A coded transmission that we can't decode," Boxer commented to Cowly.

"Russian?"

"COMMO wouldn't commit himself."

"He's being extra cautious," Cowly said. "But he's developed a sixth sense about it—something to do with the way the message is transmitted."

Boxer keyed the COMMO. "Tell me about the way the message was transmitted. Cowly says you've developed a sixth sense."

"You're going to think me crazy."

"Maybe."

"If I didn't know the *T* went down, I'd guess that message was sent from the *T*, or from the same radio equipment that she had aboard."

"We can check that when we reach port," Boxer said.

"How?"

"The Company would know what equipment was aboard the *T* and it would be easy for them to find out what other ships have identical radios."

"Will you let me know, Skipper?"

"Sure thing," Boxer answered. He looked at Cowly. "What do you think?"

Cowly shrugged.

"Yeah, that's the way I feel about it," Boxer said.

When the *Shark* was tied up, Trish was on the pier waiting for him. This time she didn't ask to come aboard and Boxer didn't ask her.

In less than a half hour, Boxer signed off the *Shark* and joined Trish. "Thanks for coming," he said.

"I was so angry when I left you," she said, "I wasn't going to. But I've had three days to calm down." She turned on the ignition and burned rubber.

"You still seem to be angry," Boxer said.

"And you don't seem to be in the least bit contrite," she answered.

"I think we have to talk," Boxer said. "I mean, really talk."

"That suits me fine," Trish answered.

Boxer filled his pipe, lit it and said, "I'd rather wait until we reach the apartment."

Trish nodded, but didn't answer.

The mobile phone rang.

Trish answered it. "It's my grandfather. He wants to speak to you."

"Yes," Boxer said.

"There's a meeting in my office at eleven hundred tomorrow morning," Kinkade said.

"I'll be there."

"Anything I should know?"

"Nothing. But I would appreciate it if you had someone on your staff run a check for me."

"What kind of a check?"

"I want to know what ships used by the Company, or commercially, have the same kind of radio equipment that was aboard the *Tecumseh*."

"I don't have to run a check. I can tell you. It was one of a kind—custom designed and built."

Boxer shifted in the bucket seat. Though the car was air-conditioned, he could feel the beads of sweat form on his brow and back. "Are you absolutely certain?" he asked.

"I approved the expenditures for it. Much of it has a top secret classification."

Boxer puffed hard on his pipe. He decided not to say anything to Kinkade about the coded message until the meeting the following morning.

"What the hell is that all about?" Kinkade asked.

"See you at eleven hundred," Boxer said, ignoring the question. "Good night." He replaced the phone in its cradle and leaning back on the head rest he closed his eyes. His stomach suddenly felt like a huge knot. Something was wrong, very wrong.

"Have you eaten dinner?" Trish asked.

He opened his eyes and caught her glancing at him. "Right now I couldn't eat a thing. But I sure as hell could use a drink."

"Why didn't you say so," she answered. "There are some places along the road."

Boxer closed his eyes again. The message from the *Trade Wind* came back into his thoughts. Something was wrong with that too. Something—He opened his eyes, sat up, picked up the phone and dialed the *Shark*'s assigned telephone number.

"Lieutenant Brock," a man said.

"Captain Boxer, the *Shark*'s skipper."

"Yes sir."

"I want a two man guard detail, twenty four hours a day at the COMMOCENTER."

"I don't have the authority—"

"I do. Contact base Hq. Tell them I gave the order."

"Roger that," Brock said.

"If there's no guard, it's your ass, Lieutenant," Boxer said sharply. "Roger that?"

"Roger it," Brock answered.

"What was that all about?" Trish asked.

Boxer replaced the phone. He wondered how much he should tell her and decided the less she knew the better. "I just don't want anyone in the communications center," he said.

After a few moments Trish answered, "I don't buy it . . . but if that's what you want to tell, then that's all you'll tell me. Right?"

"Right," Boxer said.

He closed his eyes again and leaned back on the headrest. All kinds of thoughts about what might have happened to the *T* whirled through his mind.

"Are you sure you still want to stop for a drink?" Trish asked.

"Yes, absolutely sure," Boxer said. He took a deep breath and for the first time since he got into the car, he became aware of Trish's perfume. It was delicate, yet provocative. "You smell good," he told her.

73

"Thanks. For a while there, I wasn't sure you knew I was here."

Boxer put his hand on her thigh and gently squeezed it. He could feel the warmth of her flesh through the slacks. "I know you're here," he said, opening his eyes and looking at her. She was wearing a white head band, a white blouse and white slacks. Suddenly an enormous wave of tenderness welled up inside of him and he leaned over and gently kissed her on the cheek.

"What's that for?"

Boxer settled back in his seat. "A spontaneous gesture of tenderness," he said, lighting his pipe again.

Trish glanced at him but remained silent.

Boxer switched on the radio. The sound of a string quartet filled the car. "That's Borodine's kind of music," he commented; then to Trish, he said, "You'd like him. He's got a rough road ahead, a real rough one."

"Because you rescued him?"

"His wife—the woman who was going to be his wife— was killed in an accident on the way to the hospital to give birth to their child."

"That's a rough one, alright," Trish agreed. "How was he when you left him?"

Boxer shrugged. "Hard to know. The last few minutes we almost had another shooting incident."

"Why?"

Boxer shrugged. Though she had seen Dr. Kassov being escorted off the *Shark*, he couldn't tell her anything about the man. Any information about the doctor had to come from the Company. "Just one of those things that happens," Boxer said evasively.

Trish didn't pursue the subject and they drove for a few minutes in silence.

Boxer listened to the music, trying hard not to think about the *Tecumseh*.

"There's a place," Trish said.

"Good. I'm beginning to feel hungry," Boxer answered.

Trish slowed down, turned into the gravel parking area. "Must be good . . . It's crowded."

"Come to think of it," Boxer said, "the last time I remember having something to eat was this morning. At least that was the last time I was in the mess area."

"God, you're impossible!" Trish exclaimed, as she pulled into an open area between two cars and stopped.

"No comment," Boxer said, opening the door and getting out of the car. He went around to the other side, opened the door and helped Trish out. "Kind of a rustic place," he said, taking hold of her hand.

A few minutes later they were seated at a table near a large window that overlooked a strand of woods. A candle in the middle of the table gave off a flickering yellow light. Two rooms away a three piece band played the latest songs and couples gyrated on a small dance floor.

When the waitress came to the table, Boxer ordered a Stoli on the rocks for himself and a Rob Roy for Trish.

"It's too noisy here," Trish complained.

Boxer agreed.

"Let's have our drinks and go somewhere else," Trish suggested.

Boxer took hold of her hand. "You know we have to talk."

She nodded. "I'm a little afraid of what you're going to say."

"I feel the same way," Boxer said.

"I don't believe you're afraid of anything."

"If you believe that, then you also believe the moon is made of cheese. Of course I'm afraid. I've just learned to control it."

"Are you controlling it now?"

"You better believe it," Boxer answered.

The waitress brought their drinks.

Boxer raised his glass. "To us," he toasted.

"To us," Trish echoed, touching her glass to Boxer's. They drank.

"One more toast," Boxer said.

"Make it."

"Comrade Captain Igor Borodine—may luck and happiness be yours," Boxer said, raising his glass again.

Trish touched Boxer's glass and repeated what he said.

"Now about us," Boxer said, after they drank.

"It's hard to share you," Trish told him, looking down at the white table cloth.

Boxer pursed his lips. He was never any good at explaining his relationship to his boat and to the men he commanded. Years before he had tried to explain it to Gwen and had failed. The only woman who understood without having to be told was Cynthia. That was because her family was Navy, and she herself was an officer.

"I'm a selfish woman," Trish said softly. "I'm used to getting what I want, when I want it. I wanted you so badly that I seduced you into fucking me in your cabin. I wanted you so badly because I was beginning to feel that the *Shark* had more of you than I ever did, than I ever would."

"You're confusing—"

"No, Jack, let me finish. I know several writers and artists. Their wives and sweethearts only have a part of them. The rest of what they are is devoted to what they do. The more dedicated they are to their art, the less they have for the people around them. In that way you and my ex-husband are identical. He is totally committed to—"

"That's not a flattering comparison," Boxer said.

She squeezed his hand. "The comparison was in one area only. You know what I think of you as a lover."

Boxer smiled. "Tell me. It's good for my ego."

"When it comes to making love, your ego is big enough."

76

The waitress returned to the table and asked them if they were ready to order.

"Trish, what will you have?" Boxer asked.

"I had dinner hours ago . . . But you order," she said.

"I'd like an end cut of roast beef," Boxer said, "a baked potato and a salad with blue cheese dressing."

"Anything to drink?" the waitress asked.

"A refill on this," Boxer said, holding up the glass. "What about you, Trish?"

"Yes, I'd like another," she answered.

"Now it's my turn to speak," Boxer said.

"Your turn."

"I give you as much of myself as I can," Boxer said. "I love you . . . I want you . . . I want to share my life with you. But I also have another love—my work. That work requires me to care for the men who are under my command. Trish, those men are part of me and I am part of them."

"That's what I have difficulty dealing with," she said. "I saw that on Cowly's face when he was in the doorway watching us fuck. That man is in love with you."

"Cowly is a special case," Boxer said. "But in some ways he's not. The danger that we share draws all of us together. The bond between us is very strong— In many ways stronger than any of the bonds the men have ashore. This last trip out—" He stopped himself.

"Go on, tell me . . . Share it with me!"

Boxer shook his head. "It doesn't belong with you, Trish." He gestured with his right hand. "It has nothing to do with a roadhouse restaurant on Saturday night. It *is* Saturday night, isn't it?"

"Yes."

"I'm not being difficult, or mysterious," Boxer said. "It's just that I live in two very different worlds. Try to understand that. One world is you, making love to you, doing things together, having dinner in a roadside

77

restaurant. The other—" he paused for a few moments; then he said, "is hunting and being hunted."

"I know; it's very dangerous," she commented in a low voice.

The waitress returned with their refills. "Your roast beef will be out soon," she said.

Boxer nodded and when she was gone, he said, "I can't tell you anything more."

Trish took hold of his hand and kissed it. "I'll try to come to terms with it," she said.

"If you can't—"

"I don't want to think about that possibility."

"Trish," Boxer said, "I don't want to make you unhappy and I don't want to be unhappy."

"I know that."

Boxer reached across the table and ran his hand down the left side of Trish's face. "You have to make all the adjustments," he said gently. "I can't make any. If I could, I would."

"I love you," Trish said kissing the palm of his hand.

"Later, I'll show just how much I love you," Boxer answered.

"Tell me how you'll do it," she teased.

Boxer shook his head. "That'll spoil it."

"It'll make it all the better."

"No way," Boxer said, grinning. "You'll just have to wait until the real thing happens."

Seven

Boxer awoke. The drawn venetian shades cast the bedroom in a demilight. He looked at the digital clock on the night table next to him. It was 8:05.24. He reached over the clock to the phone and picked it up. Quickly, he punched out the number he wanted.

"Headquarters motorpool . . . Warrant Officer Jenkins here."

"This is Captain Boxer . . . Is PO Paul Zweky on duty today?"

"No, sir . . . But if you want him, he could be ordered in."

"No that won't be necessary today," Boxer said. "But I want him assigned to me until further notice."

"Yes, sir."

"Have him report to me tomorrow at ten hundred hours," Boxer said.

"Does he know where to go?"

"Yes," Boxer answered. "And thanks, Jenkins."

Boxer put the phone down and got out of bed. He was completely naked.

"What was that all about?" Trish asked.

Boxer turned to her. The light blanket was below her bare breasts. Her long blond hair cascaded over the lavender colored pillow. "I want to get back to the *Shark* before my meeting with Kinkade—I mean your grandfather."

"I'll drive you," she said, pushing herself up on her elbows. The blanket fell away. Like Boxer, she too was completely naked.

Boxer shook his head. "I'll arrange for a 'Copter to fly me out and back to Langly."

She stretched languorously. "Was it good for you last night?"

"Very—and you?"

"I feel as if I've been reborn," she said, lifting her arms toward him.

Boxer bent down and kissed her on the mouth and at the same time fondled her breasts.

"Come back to bed for awhile," she purred.

"If I do, I'll never get to the *Shark*. Com'on. Get up and we'll have breakfast together before I leave."

"I'm offering something better than breakfast," she said in a low throaty voice.

"Breakfast will do just fine," he said drawing away from her.

"You're a mean man," Trish chided.

"Absolutely," he said and taking hold of the blanket, he pulled it away from her. "Now up!"

"You sure you don't want to breakfast on something else before you—"

"It'll be there when I come back," Boxer said, padding off to the bathroom.

"What makes you so sure of that?" she called from the bedroom.

"Because I treat it real good," he answered, and began to shave. A half hour later he was dressed and seated opposite Trish at the table.

"Bacon and eggs or—"

"Toast and coffee will be more than enough," Boxer said. "I have to be at the Washington airport in an hour."

"If you don't eat," she said, "how do you expect to keep your strength up?"

"That's not really what you want me to keep up," Boxer said matter of factly.

Trish stuck out her tongue. "You're mighty sure of yourself, aren't you?"

"Yes, very," Boxer answered.

Trish came alongside of him and poured coffee into his cup.

Boxer put his arm around her waist. She wasn't wearing anything more than a diaphanous negligée. He drew her to him and pressed his face against her midriff.

She gasped and in a throaty voice, she said, "Watch out or I'll spill the coffee over you."

Boxer released her.

"Do you think we'll be having dinner with my grandfather?" she asked, sitting down.

"I would imagine so," Boxer said, finishing his coffee. "Listen, I've got to run."

"Then run!"

Boxer started for the door, came back and tilting her face up, he kissed her on the lips. "Tomorrow we'll spend the day together, I promise you."

Trish grimaced.

"My word of honor," Boxer said; then he turned and left the apartment.

Stark and Williams were already in Kinkade's office when Boxer arrived. He shook hands with both men before sitting down in the empty chair facing Kinkade.

"Any particular reason why you took a 'Copter out to the *Shark* this morning?" Kinkade asked.

Boxer reached into the envelope he carried and took out two reels of tape. "These," he said. "One has the coded message we can't decipher, and the other has a request from the Coast Guard Cutter *Trade Wind* for our position."

81

"But that request never should have been made," Kinkade said.

"That's right," Boxer answered. "It never should have been made."

"Stark, whoever that captain is, I want him—" Kinkade began.

"It wasn't made by the captain of the *Trade Wind*," Boxer said.

Williams leaned slightly forward. "Then who would make such a request?"

"The same people who sent the coded message," Boxer said. "My communications officer—"

"What Boxer is trying to tell us," Kinkade said, "is that he doesn't believe the *Tecumseh* was sunk."

"I think if you'll have the two messages analyzed, you'll find they were sent from identical transmitters and since the transmitter aboard *Tecumseh* was one of a kind, it would be impossible for her to be sunk and still transmit two different messages."

"That would account for no wreckage and no survivors," Williams said.

Boxer nodded.

"Piracy?"

"Certainly," Stark answered. "But was the *Tecumseh* chosen because of what she is, or was the choice more arbitrary?"

"How the hell can they hope to hide a ship of that size?" Kinkade asked.

"It can be done," Stark said. "Make a few structural changes. Change the name, give her a new paint job and she'll look like a different vessel."

"I remember something like that going on in the early eighties," Williams said. "If I'm not mistaken, a freighter was involved."

"It *was* a freighter," Stark said. "But I can't remember its name."

"Suppose Boxer is right—" Kinkade started to say.

"The tapes will prove me right," Boxer said.

Kinkade continued, "What are we going to do about it?"

"The truth is, not very much," Stark said. "We can't stop every supertanker and examine its radio equipment. We can't even monitor the transmissions from all of them at the same time. And there's no guarantee that the radio equipment wouldn't be replaced."

"My God," Williams suddenly exclaimed, "just think of the amount of information they now have! All the operating instructions and repair manuals for the *Shark*—the code books. It's a major loss!"

"It certainly is," Boxer agreed.

"The real question," Boxer said, "is: who has the *Tecumseh*?"

"We haven't had an act of piracy on our coasts for over a hundred years," Kinkade responded.

"Then we have to assume the Russians have her," Williams said.

"I'd say so," Stark said.

"Then she'll make for one of their ports to be altered," Kinkade commented.

"Probably," Boxer said.

"There are only two, possibly three ports that can handle a ship that size. I'll alert our agents."

"That takes care of Russian ports," Boxer said, "but suppose she puts into another port and is altered there. If that should be the case, we're dealing several dozen ports, not just two or three. And if I were the Ruskie in charge of the operation, that's just what I'd have the *Tecumseh* do. I'd use a foreign port and keep her as far away from Russia as possible, at least until she's altered."

Kinkade nodded. "That makes sense."

"But it wouldn't hurt to cover the Russian ports," Boxer said.

"I don't see that we can do much but wait and see what happens," Stark said.

"At least we can assume that Rugger and his men are alive," Kinkade said.

"Maybe, maybe not," Boxer said. "That would depend on how much of a fight they put up when the *Tecumseh* was boarded, or whether or not the man in command had orders to kill them. There are too many variables to assume anything about them. We just don't know."

"Does anyone have anything more to say about the *Tecumseh*?" Kinkade asked. "No. Alright, we can get on to new business." He looked at Stark. "Have you told him anything yet?"

Boxer's stomach suddenly tightened.

"Nothing," Stark said.

Kinkade rested his elbows on the top of the desk. "We have a new assignment coming up for you—one that should not take more than two weeks at the very most. We have a new type submarine that is designed for a combination ocean and river operation. It will be used to bring an assault team up a river, wait until the team has accomplished its mission, then evacuate them. Once it's back in the open ocean it can submerge to a depth one thousand feet. Naturally, it is armed with torpedos."

"And how will it defend itself on the river?" Boxer asked, his voice on the thin edge of anger.

"She has two turrets with rapid firing five inchers," Stark said.

"Two turrets?"

"She's as well armed for surface operations as any frigate," Stark said.

"Well, that gives me something of a fighting chance to at least stay alive," Boxer answered.

"Why don't you come by my office in a few days and take a look at the specs," Stark said.

"When does this assignment start?"

"We want you on station by the end of the month," Kinkade answered.

"And that includes sea trials?"

"The operation will be part of the sea trials," Stark said.

"That doesn't give me or my men much of a margin in case—"

"We don't have any margin," Kinkade said. "You're going to bring out a group of prisoners."

"Prisoners? From where?"

"You won't know that until you're well out to sea. Your orders will be opened twenty-four hours after you leave port."

Boxer looked questioningly at Stark.

"It must be that way, Jack," Stark said.

"Do I use my own crew and Vargas's team, or am I going to break in a new crew and go with a new team?"

"In addition to yourself," Kinkade said, "you'll need nineteen men. Half will be off the *Shark* and half will be new. That's just operating personnel. Another twenty men will be needed to man the various weapon systems."

"And the assault team?"

"Take Vargas and four others. The rest of the team will be new men."

"How many in the rest of the team?" Boxer asked.

"Four twenty-five man units—all have been training for the last six months."

"But all of them are cherry; they have never been in combat."

Kinkade nodded.

"A new boat, half a new crew, and a completely new assault team. I don't see how I could fail," Boxer commented sarcastically.

"If you fail, you'll be killed or captured," Kinkade said.

"Kinkade, unless you haven't realized it until now,

I've been there before. I lost men this last time out."

"I don't want to get into that now," Kinkade said.
"You're responsible for the loss of those men and—"

Boxer was out of his seat.

"Sit down, Captain!" Stark snapped.

Boxer hesitated.

Stark nodded.

"You owe Captain Boxer an apology Kinkade," Stark said.

"If—"

"You owe Captain Boxer an apology," Stark repeated, his voice harder than the first time.

Kinkade nodded. "I apologize, Captain."

Boxer was still too angry to speak.

"There's one more item," Stark said.

Boxer took a deep breath and slowly exhaled before he said, "Tell me what it is."

"Captain Bush is going with you."

"That fucking cuts it!" Boxer exclaimed, getting to his feet once more. "He's going but I'm not."

"Both of you are going," Stark said.

"Admiral, we just don't work—"

"That's bullshit," Stark said in his gravelly voice. "The record shows you work well together. You don't agree, but you have always gotten results—very good ones I might add."

"Bush is a rigid bastard."

"But you yourself commended him for his bravery," Kinkade said.

"You don't understand. He has to be able to handle men . . . He has to be flexible."

"He goes and you go," Stark said. "You have total command. Bush won't interfere with you or your EXO, but he needs the experience."

"What experience? He'll be nothing more than an observer."

"That's right. But he'll be where the action is."

"I want it in writing that Bush has absolutely no authority aboard—what the hell is the boat's name?"

"No name yet . . . Just number sixty-nine," Williams said.

"At least I like the number," Boxer responded straight-faced.

Stark suppressed a smile. "Okay, you'll get it in writing."

Eight

The sun was shining and though it was the middle of June, Moscow was still cool. Holding two red roses in his hands, Borodine stood at the foot of the still raw mound of earth that covered Irena. It was hard for him to accept the fact that he would never see her again, never delight in her body, and never hear the sound of her voice.

"I loved you," he said silently and he placed one of the red roses where her breasts would be. Then taking a deep breath, he slowly exhaled and moved a step to the right where there was a much smaller mound of raw earth.

He had been told by the hospital authorities that the child had been a boy. "She hadn't decided what your name would have been, but I think she was leaning toward Dimitri," he said, still speaking silently. And he added, "I know we would have been good friends." He knelt down and placed the rose in the middle of the mound; then he stood up and using a handkerchief, he wiped his eyes and blew his nose.

"I won't forget either of you," Borodine whispered and when he turned to go, he saw Viktor and the entire crew of the *Sea Savage* standing a respectful distance behind him. Suslov and the other scientists were there too. All of them carried flowers.

Deeply touched, Borodine couldn't move.

Viktor came toward him, nodded and placed some of

the flowers that he held on Irena's grave and some on the child's. One by one the men of the *Sea Savage* followed; then Suslov came and the scientists followed.

Clearing his throat, Borodine said, "Thank you. . . . Thank you."

Viktor stepped forward. "You didn't think we'd let you come here alone, did you?"

Borodine shook his head. "I didn't think about it . . . I—" He couldn't continue to speak.

Viktor embraced him. "Come, comrade; we have provided the traditional funeral feast."

Borodine allowed himself to be led out of the cemetery and to a waiting car.

"Doctor Suslov has permitted us to use her house, and the men have provided the money for the food and the vodka," Viktor said, as they settled into the car.

Viktor drove.

"How will the men get to the house?"

"Some of my friends have friends in the transportation section. Four buses have been assigned to me."

"It's good to have friends, Viktor," Borodine said, "very good."

After a few moments of silence, Viktor asked, "Have you seen Comrade Admiral Goshkov yet?"

"Tomorrow morning," Borodine answered.

"I was already warned not to speak about the *Storozhevoy* to anyone except authorized individuals," Viktor said.

Borodine closed his eyes and leaned back.

"The rest of the crew received the same warning," Viktor explained.

"I was warned too," Borodine responded.

Neither man spoke again until Viktor announced, "We're here!"

Borodine opened his eyes. They had stopped in front of a lovely brick house located somewhere in the outskirts of Moscow. "That belongs to her?" Borodine asked, surprised at the size of the house and the plot of land on which it stood.

"Louisa Suslov is an important person," Viktor commented.

"Obviously," Borodine answered.

The two men started up the walkway just as Louisa turned into the driveway.

"I had better go and thank her," Borodine said.

Viktor nodded.

Borodine went to Louisa's car and opened the door for her.

She smiled up at him.

"Let me help you," he said, offering her his hand.

"I love driving it," she said. "But it's difficult to get in and out of it, especially with a skirt or dress on." As soon as she began to move, the hem of her dress moved up.

"Yes, I can see that," Borodine answered, looking down at her bare thighs.

She flushed.

"Free and clear!" Borodine exclaimed when she was out of the car and on her feet.

"I have something I want to ask you," Louisa said, wrapping her arm around his.

"Not before I thank you for this," Borodine responded. "It was very kind of you."

"I knew that if I didn't do it, it wouldn't be done. Besides, it's really a very small payment for what you did for me."

"I—"

"You saved all of our lives," she said in a low throaty voice.

Borodine shook his head. "It wasn't me who rescued us. It was Comrade Captain Boxer."

"An absolutely remarkable man," she said.

"You know I agree with that," Borodine replied.

"Can you tell me why he kissed me?" Louisa asked.

Borodine flashed back a smile. He looked straight at her. She was an attractive woman. "It was his way of saying goodby," Borodine answered.

"Nothing more?"

Borodine shrugged.

Louisa lowered her eyes. "He kissed me open mouth," she said. "A man doesn't do that unless he wants to sleep with the woman he kissed."

"Perhaps," Borodine said, "he was saying that in a different set of circumstances he would have tried."

Louisa nodded. "Yes, that's what I think. He would have tried."

"And would you have gone to bed with him?"

She flushed again.

"The truth," Borodine pressed. He remembered her telling him that she had several lovers, but now she almost looked like an innocent girl.

"Yes," she answered. "I would have."

"Maybe someday you'll meet him and the circumstances will be more favorable."

"Now you're making fun of me," she said.

"Absolutely not," Borodine assured her.

She shook her head. "It will never happen," she said. "There is practically no chance of us meeting again."

"Probably not," Borodine agreed. "But then again it might."

"I'll tell you something else," Louisa said. "Even if I never see him again, I will never forget him."

Borodine patted her hand. "I know what you mean," he said.

Admiral Goshkov, flanked by Vice Admiral Vorshilov on his right and General Krotkov, the Deputy Commander of the KGB on his left were at one end of the table.

Vorshilov was a heavy set man with submarine experience, though none of it had ever been in combat. The general was tall, thin and gray.

Borodine sat at the other end of the table, with Viktor on his right and Suslov to his left. The previous day neither of them had mentioned, or even hinted, that they would be at the hearing. But then he realized they had been warned not to tell him. Like him they wore their uniforms.

Borodine had spent the first hour explaining the events that lead to the sinking of the *Sea Savage*.

"Everything you have told us," Admiral Vorshilov said, "is covered in the operational tapes and your subsequent report. But you said very little about the effectiveness of the killer darts."

"They are extremely effective," Borodine said. "There was no way I could escape being hit by them."

"But escape is possible, isn't it?" Vorshilov asked.

Borodine knew that the admiral was referring to Boxer's escape. "Under certain circumstances I would have to answer yes to your question. Comrade Captain Boxer proved that it could be done."

"But you could not find the circumstances to save your boat?" Vorshilov challenged.

"I could not," Borodine answered, "and with all due respect Comrade Admiral, I doubt if you could have, had you been aboard. Comrade Boxer had the advantage of having two very fast minisubs, which he used with stunning effectiveness."

Admiral Goshkov cleared his throat. "The purpose of the sea darts is to kill submarines. Comrade Captain Boxer had no means of countering them."

Vorshilov nodded and glanced at General Krotkov.

"I am particularly interested in your attempt, Comrade Captain, to take over the *Shark*," Krotkov said. "According, to your own words, you were against it."

"That is true."

"Why?"

"We were not prisoners," Borodine answered. "We were survivors."

"Oh? I was under the impression that you and the Comrade Captain Boxer had fought one another on several different occasions?"

Borodine nodded.

"Then you were prisoners—"

"Absolutely not . . . Not until the attempt to take over the *Shark* failed."

"Comrade General," Suslov said, "perhaps I might be able to clarify the point under discussion."

"Please, Colonel, I'd appreciate it if you did," Krotkov said.

"Comrade Captain Boxer treated all of the survivors with courtesy and respect. The rescue itself was a remarkable feat and done at great risk to the men who accomplished it."

"I do understand that," Krotkov answered.

"The problem, Colonel," Admiral Goshkov said, "is why, if Comrade Captain Boxer considered you survivors and not prisoners, he felt it necessary to destroy the *Sea Savage?*"

"Had the situation been reversed," Borodine answered, "I would have destroyed the *Shark*."

"Alright," Krotkov said, "suppose you had rescued the *Shark*'s crew, would you have considered them prisoners, or survivors?"

Without hesitating, Borodine answered, "Survivors."

Krotkov's face remained expressionless. "Were you on the bridge of the *Shark* when it was engaged in combat with several of our surface ships?" he questioned.

Borodine nodded.

"Then am I to understand that you helped Comrade Borodine sink and/or badly damage several of our ships?" Krotkov asked.

"Those ships were out to sink the *Shark*," Borodine said tightly. He knew he was on very, very thin ice.

"That, Comrade Captain, is an admission of treason," Krotkov responded sharply.

"My crew was in danger of being killed," Borodine answered. "Had there been another way, I would have taken it."

For several moments, no one at the table spoke.

"I have one more question Comrade Captain," Krotkov said.

Borodine nodded.

"According to your report you gave Comrade Captain Boxer the position of the undersea cave that—"

"Yes," Borodine said. "It would have provided protection from the surface ships."

"But it wasn't needed, was it?"

"It wasn't needed."

"But Comrade Captain Boxer took the *Shark* into it and then realizing that it might be used for a submarine base, he destroyed it."

"Yes," Borodine answered.

"I am not at all sure I understand your actions," Krotkov said.

Borodine flushed. "My actions, Comrade General, were dictated by responsibility to save my crew."

"I will vouch for that," Suslov added.

"And so will I," Viktor added.

"I have another question," Admiral Vorshilov said. "According to your report, Comrade Captain Boxer threatened to fire at the fishing trawler if any member of its crew interfered with Doctor Kassov's defection. Is that correct?"

"Yes. That is correct," Borodine answered.

"What *did* you, and what *do* you, think about that threat?"

"Given the circumstances," Borodine said, "I understood it then, and I understand it now."

"Do you condone it?"

"I would have done the same thing," Borodine said.

"It seems, Comrade Captain, you are somewhat confused about—"

Borodine was on his feet. "I am not confused about anything regarding my duty, or my responsibility. If anyone is confused, Comrade Admiral, it is you and the Comrade General. The nature of my assignment does not permit me the luxury of following rules and regulations. I must operate as I see fit. I must make decisions that will protect my crew and my boat. This time I could not save my boat, but I was able to bring back my entire crew, with the exception of those who were killed during our encounter with the *Storozhevoy* and those who were killed in the unsuccessful attempt to take over the *Shark*. I am neither ashamed of what I did, nor guilty of treason as was said. I do not think any officer at this table, with the exception of myself, Comrade Commander Korsenko and Colonel Suslov have any idea what conditions were like on either the *Sea Savage* or the *Shark*." He stopped and took a deep breath. He could feel his heart racing.

"Am I to understand, Comrade Captain, that you consider yourself above following rules and regulations?" General Krotkov asked.

"Only when they have no application to the situation," Borodine answered hotly. He looked at Viktor and Suslov. Both of them were very pale.

Krotkov nodded. "I have no more questions," he said.

"Neither do I," Admiral Vorshilov said.

"You are excused Comrade Captain Borodine," Admiral Goshkov said.

Borodine saluted the three officers. Certain that in a few hours, he'd be arrested and charged with treason, he turned on his heel and quickly left the room.

*   *   *

Admiral Goshkov declared a ten minute recess and ordered coffee and small sugared buns be brought to the table. He and Vorshikov smoked long cuban cigars. He spent a few minutes chatting with Suslov about the weather and, when he was sure that everyone had at least one cup of coffee and one bun, he reconvened the hearing.

"This time," Gorshkov said, "I have several questions I want to ask. First, Comrade Commander Korsenko, you have been given the opportunity to command your own boat, yet you chose to remain aboard the *Q-Twenty One.* Will you tell us why?"

"Comrade Captain Borodine is the best submarine captain we have," Viktor said. "The fact that the *Sea Savage* was sunk does not reflect on his ability to command. We did not have an effective defense against the sea darts, nor did we have the means to improvise one, as Comrade Captain Boxer had."

"And you have no criticism of his other actions?" Goshkov asked.

Viktor shook his head. "None, Comrade Admiral."

"You would have done exactly what he has done?"

Viktor hesitated.

"Answer the Comrade Admiral's question," General Krotkov barked.

"Please, Comrade General, allow the man the time necessary to weigh his answer," Goshkov said sharply.

Viktor looked straight at Goshkov. "I would not have the courage to do what he has done, not only on the last mission, but on every mission we carried out. Comrade Captain Borodine and his American counterpart are the most courageous men I know."

"Then you agree with him on his attitude toward the rules and regulations?" Goshkov asked.

Again Viktor nodded. "Rules and regulations are for

ordinary circumstances but we were in extraordinary circumstances."

"Comrade Commander Korsenko, thank you for your honesty," Goshkov said; then he turned his attention to Suslov. "Comrade Colonel, you were present at all times during the *Q-Twenty One*'s last cruise?"

"Yes, Comrade Admiral," Suslov answered.

"I would like your opinion on everything you saw and heard."

"Comrade Captain Borodine's actions cannot, in my opinion, be faulted."

"But according to his report," Goshkov said, "you had violent objections to several things he did."

"Yes that is true," Suslov answered. "But I did not understand the overall picture, which, of course, was to bring as many of us as possible back to Russia."

"Then you too think he had reasons to disregard the rules and regulations that govern other naval officers?"

"Yes. The situation in which we found ourselves was unique," Suslov answered.

"Did you consider yourself a prisoner aboard the *Shark*?"

"Only when our attempt to capture it failed," Suslov answered. "Then Comrade Captain Boxer had no choice but to put us and keep us under armed guard."

"Thank you, Comrade Colonel, for your cooperation," Goshkov said with a smile. "You and Comrade Commander Korsenko have been most helpful. The two of you are excused."

Viktor and Suslov stood up, saluted, turned smartly around, and left the room.

Goshkov waited until the door was closed before he said, "Well, gentlemen, what is your reaction to what you've read in the various reports, heard on the tapes, and heard in this room?"

"The rules and regulations must be followed," General Krotkov said.

Goshkov nodded and took the time to light another cigar before he said, "But I am not sure which rules and regulations would apply in the circumstances the Comrade Captain Borodine found himself."

"He certainly committed treason when he helped the enemy—"

"Before you continue, Comrade General, consider the following facts: he was ordered to attack and sink a Russian ship."

"Yes, but that ship was in the process of defecting," Krotkov said.

"The ship was still Russian," Goshkov answered.

"I don't see what you're getting at," Admiral Vorshilov said.

"The *Shark* was under attack by Russian surface ships. It had to defend itself. Comrade Captain Borodine was acting to defend his men. He would have been remiss in his duty if he did not make an attempt to insure the safety of his men."

"Then you are telling us that Comrade Captain Borodine was following navy rules and regulations."

"Inasmuch as he is duty bound to protect his men, yes," Goshkov answered, blowing a huge cloud of white smoke toward the ceiling. "He made no attempt to hide anything he did. Everything is either on tape or in his report."

"I think you have created a monster," General Krotkov said.

"I think so too," Admiral Vorshilov agreed.

"And so do I," Goshkov said. "But the reality of the situation in which we find ourselves is that we need monsters like Comrade Captain Borodine. We need men who can think for themselves, who use the rules and regulations in ordinary circumstances, but when the circumstances become extraordinary, they create their own rules and regulations."

"Then you would not charge him—"

Goshkov held up his hand. "I will personally reprimand him for operating too close to what might be termed treason, but I would not consider having him arrested by either the KGB or by our own security forces."

"I am sorry Comrade Admiral," General Krotkov said, "but I can't agree with you. I will present this entire matter to my superior and urge him to take appropriate actions."

"That is your right, Comrade General. But let me tell you from the very outset that I will put the full weight of the navy behind Comrade Captain Borodine's defense should it come to that."

Krotkov flushed.

"And that weight is considerable," Goshkov said calmly.

"Perhaps, I might find room for reconsideration," Krotkov said.

"Then, if I were you," Goshkov told him, "I'd find the room. I want this entire matter cleared up as quickly as possible."

"With your permission, Comrade Admiral," Krotkov said, standing, "I would like to leave."

Goshkov nodded.

Krotkov saluted the two admirals and walked quickly to the door. A moment later he was out of the room.

Goshkov turned to Vorshilov. "Arrange to have all tapes and notes of this hearing destroyed. That includes those held by the KGB."

"That might be very difficult."

"Do it!" commanded Goshkov.

*   *   *

Late that same afternoon Borodine was summoned back to Goshkov's office. He expected a cold, formal greeting and to be told to tender his resignation, or informed that he would shortly be arrested by the KGB. But instead, as soon as he entered the office, Goshkov left his desk, crossed the room and shaking his hand warmly said, "You give me more trouble than you're worth Comrade Captain."

"That is never my intention, Comrade Admiral," Borodine answered

"Come sit down," Goshkov said, "and we will talk a bit. But first I need a drink. What about you?"

"Yes, I need one too," Borodine answered. He knew he was off the hook, and suddenly he felt very tired.

"Better I know a fine restaurant and I still owe you a dinner. You thought I forgot, but you see I didn't." He went directly to his desk, picked up the phone and ordered his car be ready within five minutes.

Borodine was both pleased and confused. Earlier in the afternoon he had visions of himself being tried, convicted, and sentenced to a prison camp, or worse a rehabilitation center. The very thought of that having been a possibility, sent a shiver through him.

"Come," Goshkov commented. "It will take us at least five minutes to reach the garage." As they left the office, he said, "I am sorry for your loss. I am sorry you were notified while you were at sea. I learned of my first wife's death that way, and I know how difficult it is to take."

"Thank you, Comrade Admiral." Borodine answered.

"I cannot offer you any words of consolation," Goshkov said, as they reached the elevator, "except not to rush into any sort of deep relationship with a woman until you've let time do its work—and it will. Enjoy as many women as you can, but be very careful about falling in love."

"It will be difficult to even think about falling in love

now," Borodine replied, allowing Goshkov to enter the elevator before him.

Once they were settled in the car, Goshkov said, "Next time, if you break rules and ignore regulations, you must be less truthful about what you did. The truth could very well destroy you."

Borodine nodded.

"Our other Comrades at the table have difficulty understanding that you cannot operate in the usual way," Goshkov said. "Sometimes I, too, am more than a bit puzzled by what you do. But I trust you and, like yourself, I believe every commander's first obligation, after he carries out his mission, is to bring his ship and his crew safely home."

"Thank you Comrade Goshkov for your confidence," Borodine said.

Goshkov nodded, reached into his inside pocket and pulled out two Cuban cigars. "Smoke one of these and you'll never smoke another cigar again without remembering it."

"Thank you. I'll smoke it after dinner."

"I'll have one now, and another later," Goshkov said. He cut the end. "Do you think you could give a full description of what you saw aboard the *Shark*— instruments and controls—anything that might be useful to help us design a *Q-Twenty Two*."

"Yes," Borodine said, trying to control the sudden excitement that suddenly filled him.

"This one will be much better than the *Sea Savage* and the *Shark*," Goshkov said. "This one will give you the edge in battle."

"I will command—"

"Yes, you will command," Goshkov said. "If I didn't need you for that, do you think I would have saved your ridiculous neck Comrade Captain Borodine?"

Borodine looked at Goshkov.

101

The Admiral's face splintered into a grin; then he started to laugh.

Borodine joined him. . . .

The restaurant was far more elegant than anything Borodine could have possibly imagined existed in Russia. It occupied the ground floor of what must have been a nobleman's summer home before the Revolution. It was surrounded on three sides by woods of pine and birch and looked over a small lake.

"I come here," Goshkov said, "whenever I feel the need for self-indulgence."

Borodine finished the last delicious morsel of Chicken Kiev, and washed it down with a glass of white wine.

"Come," Goshkov said, "we'll go out on the terrace. It's lovely out there this time of the evening." He handed him a cigar. "We'll have dessert and coffee later."

Borodine, nodded, took the cigar and respectfully waited until Goshkov stood before he got to his feet.

As they walked toward the open french doors that led to the terrace, Goshkov nodded to or greeted various individuals.

Borodine was surprised at Goshkov's cordiality. He always had known the Admiral to be a gruff, no-nonsense man and yet here he was a smiling, affable individual.

"Now isn't this a spectacular view?" Goshkov asked, as they stepped out onto the veranda.

From one end to the other, the entire western sky was splashed in various shades of orange, pink and red.

"It's very beautiful," Borodine said, lighting his cigar from the match held by Goshkov.

"I am sending you to the United States," Goshkov told him.

Borodine almost let the cigar fall from his mouth.

"I want you to attend several high level conferences

on arms control, and act as an advisor to our negotiators. There will be two other advisors from the military: one from the army and one from the airforce. Both will be generals."

"Will these conferences be held in Washington?" Borodine asked.

"Yes."

"Have I your permission to contact Comrade Captain Boxer?" Borodine asked.

"I'd have been surprised if you hadn't asked," Goshkov said with a smile; then he added, "Just for the record, I understand your relationship with Comrade Boxer."

Borodine nodded. "He is an extraordinary man," Borodine said.

"And so are you Comrade Captain Borodine, which is why I have promoted you to Rear Admiral."

This time Borodine couldn't stop his mouth from opening and the cigar fell. But he managed to catch it.

"All the paperwork is completed and in a few days I will issue the order," Goshkov said.

"Comrade Admiral Goshkov this is the third time you—no the fourth time you've surprised me today. I surely thought I was going to be arrested—"

"Not while I am still Admiral of the Fleet," Goshkov said. "You're duty was to your crew, and you carried that duty out in every way."

"Thank you Comrade Admiral," Borodine answered. "Hearing you say that means a great deal to me." Suddenly, he realized that he had no one with whom he could share his good fortune and he was filled with a great sadness.

"Now let's return to the table and have dessert and coffee. The desserts here rival anything you can get in Paris," Goshkov said with a smile.

"I am sure they do," Borodine replied, falling in

alongside Goshkov.

"I recommend the ice cream strawberry shortcake," Goshkov said, as they sat down. "And the Columbian or Brazilian coffee."

"That will be fine," Borodine answered, pushing the sadness away, and hoping some of the excitement would return. It did, but it was not nearly as intense as it had been a few moments before.

"You'll leave for Washington in two months," Goshkov said. "You can have several days to yourself before you have to work on the new boat. With any luck, it should be ready around this time next year."

"Good," Borodine exclaimed. "Very good!"

When the waiter came to the table, Goshkov ordered the ice cream strawberry shortcake and Brazilian coffee for himself and Borodine.

"I am going to visit my parents," Borodine said. "I haven't seen them in over two years."

"The navy will provide your transportation," Goshkov said with a twinkle in his gray eyes. "After all, an admiral has to have certain privileges, or there'd be no purpose in being one."

"No purpose at all," Borodine responded, smiling broadly.

Nine

"Hello Cynthia," Boxer said, looking down at Stark's secretary, who was intently looking at the screen of a word processor. She was still a very beautiful woman. Blond, voluptuous, even in the white summer uniform. And a lovely face with two blue eyes that were looking up at him.

"The Admiral is expecting you," she said formally.

He noticed that she was wearing an engagement ring. "Who's the lucky man?" he asked.

"No one you know," she answered curtly.

He and Cynthia had been lovers off and on for a few years. They were living together before he began having an affair with Trish.

"I'll tell the Admiral you're here," she said, picking up the phone.

"Are you going to the briefing?" Boxer asked.

"Yes," she answered; then punched out the Admiral's number. "Captain Jack Boxer is here, sir . . . Yes, I'll send him right in." As she spoke she nodded her head toward the door.

Boxer turned, went to the door, and knocked softly.

"Come in," Stark called out in his gravelly voice.

Boxer entered Stark's office.

The Admiral was coming toward him and immediately in front of his desk was a large model.

"Good to see you, Jack," Stark said, vigorously pumping Boxer's hand. "How's Trish."

"Fine . . . but not exactly pleased that I'm going off so soon," Boxer said honestly.

"I wouldn't think so," Stark answered; then, turning toward the model, he said, "That's it. Isn't she a beauty?"

Boxer advanced toward the model and quickly looked for the scale.

"One to ten," Stark said, knowing what Boxer was looking for.

"That makes it a lot larger than I imagined it would be," Boxer said, walking around the model.

"Code named the *Sea Turtle One*," Stark said, "or *ST-One*."

Boxer stood at the bow and studied it. He didn't like its looks. It was dumpy looking. It was ugly. Neither a ship nor a sub.

"What happens to the gun turrets and bridge when she's submerged?" Boxer asked.

"I'll call Commander Lowe in to explain," Stark said. "She's our resident expert on these things. And by the way, she's going with you on the mission."

"No way!" Boxer exclaimed; then suddenly remembering who he was speaking to he said, "I'm sorry, sir, but that just came out."

Stark nodded. "She volunteered for the assignment."

"But the risks—"

"She knows the risks," Stark said. "And she knows the *Turtle* better than anyone. You're not going to have time for regular sea trials. You'll make a couple of dives and underwater runs; then you're going in. If anything goes wrong, Commander Lowe will be aboard to ID the problem and recommend repairs."

"But she's a woman," Boxer complained.

"She also happens to be an officer in the navy," Stark said.

"What will she do?"

"She'll be assigned regular ship's duties," Stark said.

Boxer remained silent.

Stark went to the door, opened it and said, "We're ready for you now Commander."

A moment later Cynthia entered the Admiral's office.

"Will you please brief Captain Boxer on the *Turtle*," Stark said, lighting a cigar and offering one to Boxer.

"To begin with she's three hundred and sixty feet long, has a beam of forty eight feet and a displacement on the surface of twenty-two thousand tons. Her maximum underwater displacement is fifty thousand tons. Her maximum operating depth is one thousand feet. Surface cruising speed is twenty-five knots; flank speed, thirty knots. Underwater her cruising speed is thirty five knots and her flank speed forty knots. She carries an operating crew of sixty five men, including ten officers and a two hundred man assault team. Her hull consists of three shells. The middle one is made of plastic that is pressure-sensitive."

"What does that mean?" Boxer asked.

"On the surface it is a viscous liquid but when the *Turtle* dives and the pressure increases, the liquid begins to change to a solid. At about four hundred feet it is completely solid."

"How does it sense the change in pressure?"

"The outer shell flexes in on it," Cynthia said.

Boxer looked questioningly at Stark.

"Commander Lowe is completely responsible for that innovation," Stark said. "I'm sure she can explain anything you want to know about it."

"I certainly can, sir," Cynthia said.

"What about the COMCOMP system malfunction net?"

"You don't have one aboard—at least not one that's hooked in to your secondary systems. It functions only on primary systems and structural problems. It's called a Systems Check, or SYSCHK."

"Tell me what happens to the gun turrets and the bridge when she dives?"

"They retract into the hull," Cynthia said, "leaving the deck clear of any obstructions."

"Torpedos?"

"Four tubes aft."

"Missiles?"

"Two retractable batteries of four surface to surface missiles with a range of one to twenty miles. Two additional ASW batteries and four surface to air missiles with a maximum altitude of forty-five thousand feet, and last, you have eight quad barrel rapid-firing thirty-seven millimeter machine guns."

"And the two turrets—what kind of rifles do they have?"

"Each turret mounts two automatically fed five inch rifles. Each can fire anything from a three inch to a five inch shell. This is made possible changing the diameter of the rifle's bore and breech opening. Each rifle can fire twenty rounds per minute."

"She seems to be well armed," Boxer said.

"She is very well armed," Stark answered; then to Cynthia he said, "Tell Captain Boxer about the special locomotion device on her."

"If you look carefully at the bottom of the model," she said, with obvious relish, "you will see what appears to be treads—and they are treads. The *Turtle* can crawl over the bottom, or come up a beach, or, if necessary, come fully out of the water to fight and then retreat into the depths again when the action is over."

"What do you think about that?" Stark asked.

Boxer nodded. "Spectacular. Absolutely spectacular!"

Stark grinned broadly.

"Do you have any more questions?" Cynthia asked.

"Several dozen," Boxer said. "But they will keep until I'm aboard."

"There are one or two more things that you should be aware of. The *Turtle* will carry four armored vehicles that are capable of being used at maximum depth of thirty feet. They are armed with ninety millimeter recoilless rifles, four anti-tank missiles, four ground to air missiles and machine guns. There is also a pressurized bay in the bow that will permit the vehicles to exit and reenter with the *Turtle* submerged in thirty feet of water."

"I'm impressed," Boxer said.

"You should be," Cynthia answered.

Stark went to his desk. "I want you aboard the *Turtle* four days from today, and at sea two days after that. You'll open your orders twenty-four hours after you clear the harbor."

"Four days doesn't give me much time to—"

"Midnight of the fourth day," Stark said.

"Yes, sir," Boxer said, glad to have a few extra hours ashore.

"That will be all, Commander," Stark said.

"Yes, sir," Cynthia answered and left the room.

Stark returned to his desk and sat down. He gestured Boxer into a chair and said, "Regardless of your relationship to Commander Lowe, she's a very good officer and knows a great deal about the *Turtle*."

"It's just that having a woman aboard complicates the lives of the men," Boxer answered. "She's just not an ordinary woman; she's a very beautiful woman."

Stark nodded. "Would it make it any easier if I assigned three or four more. I certainly have a large pool of volunteers from which to choose—all of them are highly qualified."

"Admiral, with all due respect to the women, this is a mission, not a shake down cruise. It may or it may not be

109

a piece of cake, but we won't know that until it's over."

Stark sent a large cloud of white smoke toward the ceiling. "The additional three women will be aboard when she sails."

"Aye, aye sir," Boxer answered.

"There is one more thing I thought you'd like to know," Stark said.

"What is it?"

"Captain Borodine will be coming to Washington. He'll be here by the time you return. He has been promoted to the rank of rear admiral and will be the naval advisor to the Russian negotiators at the up-coming disarmament talks this fall."

"That's great!" Boxer exclaimed.

"I thought you'd appreciate it," Stark commented.

"So he got himself promoted," Boxer said. "And he was worried that he would be reprimanded for losing the *Q-Twenty One*."

"Just watch your step when Borodine's here," Stark cautioned. "His people will be watching him, and our people will also be watching him. That means they'll be watching anyone who has anything to do with him."

Boxer nodded. "I've been there before. I know the game."

Stark smiled. "I know you know it, but even if you do, be careful. McElroy is still very much around, though not in Congress any longer, thank God."

Boxer shook his head. "Now there's a weird man!"

Stark agreed; then he said, "I'll be on the pier when you return." He stood up and extended his hand over the desk. "Good luck, Jack."

Boxer pumped Stark's hand.

"If you really want a star," Stark said offhandedly, "I'll see what I can do to get it for you."

"It would make Trish happy," Boxer said. "She's into that kind of status nonsense."

110

Stark nodded. "Then we'll try to make Trish happy."

Boxer let go of Stark's hand, glanced at the *Turtle*; then nodding to Stark, he said, "Something like that clanking up a beach would be enough to scare the shit out of most people."

"Take it from me," Stark replied, "she can also do a lot of fancy fighting."

"When I come back, I'll let you know what she does best: scare the enemy to death or fight him," Boxer told him.

"You do that," Stark said.

Boxer went to the door, opened it, and with a final nod to Stark, he left the Admiral's office.

Boxer unlocked the door to the apartment, opened it and found himself looking past the foyer into the living room at two well-dressed men, to whom Trish was serving coffee. As Boxer entered the room, the two men stood up. Both of them were Latin types.

"Darling," Trish said, "these men have been waiting for you for almost an hour."

"Capitan," the taller of the two said, pronouncing the word with a definite Spanish accent, "Senor Sanchez—" he glanced at Trish.

"Senor Sanchez wants to see me?"

The two men nodded vigorously.

"Have your coffee and we'll go," Boxer told them; then to Trish he said, "I'll be back in a couple of hours."

The two men looked at one another. Now it was the shorter one who spoke. "He is in New York."

"New York!" Trish exclaimed.

Suddenly Boxer understood; he had asked Sanchez to find the muggers who were responsible for the death of his mother and Sanchez had.

"That's a marvelous idea. Let's go to New York,"

111

Trish said.

"This is business," Boxer said.

"But—"

"By the very latest," Boxer said, "I'll be back tomorrow morning and then we will have three days—"

Her brow furrowed.

"Don't say anything now," Boxer said. "As soon as I'm back we'll take off somewhere. Now, if you don't mind, I'd like a cup of coffee too."

"I could be ready in five minutes." Trish said.

Boxer shook his head.

"Living with you is like living with a magician," Trish said. "You're always disappearing."

Boxer finished drinking his coffee and said to the two men, "Will you excuse us for a few minutes?"

The men nodded in unison.

Boxer took hold of Trish's arm and gently moved her into the bedroom. "Listen," he said, "New York is out of the question. I'll explain everything when I come back."

She pouted. "Then you'll only be back for three days. I'm going to talk to grandfather—"

"No!" Boxer exclaimed, his voice suddenly hard. "Your relationship with him is one thing; mine is something different altogether."

"Don't bully me!"

Boxer shook his head. "I'm not! I never want you to cross certain lines on my behalf. I don't care much for your grandfather, and he sure as hell feels the same way about me. But now the two of us have you in common so we have an uneasy peace between us. I don't ever want him to do anything for me because you asked him to."

"God, you're an impossible man!" Trish exclaimed in exasperation

Boxer put his arms around her. "I'll be back as quickly as I can," he said, drawing her to him and kissing her on the lips.

112

She opened her mouth and gave him her tongue.

Boxer separated from her. "I've got to go now. See you soon," he told her, and leaving the bedroom, he said to the two men, "I'm ready to go now."

Boxer and the two men climbed aboard a Lear jet at Washington's International Airport and forty two minutes later landed in LaGuardia, on the north edge of Queens.

A stretch Limo drove them to Winthrop Street in Brooklyn. The driver was in radio contact with someone else.

The tall man, whose name Boxer had learned during the flight to New York was Edwardo, said, "They are in number forty-four on the top floor, apartment B."

"How many?" Boxer asked as they slowly drove past the four floor walk up.

"Three."

"Are they all there now?" Boxer asked, glancing at his watch. It was six o'clock in the evening.

"Si, they are there. One lives there with his woman. His brother also lives there and a third is a friend, who sleeps on a cot in the kitchen and with the woman, when the other two are not there."

"Is the house being watched?" Boxer asked.

The shorter of the two men, who answered to the name Miguel, said, "From a van parked across from it."

"I don't want to do anything now," Boxer said. "We'll wait a few hours; then we'll pay them a visit."

Both men agreed that it was best to wait.

"Now," Edwardo said, "there are too many people in the street."

And Miguel added, "We will change cars before we come back."

Boxer suggested they go for dinner. "We might as well

113

enjoy ourselves while we're waiting. There are some restaurants—"

"Captain," Edwardo said, "we would be honored if you would be our guest."

"Okay, I'm your guest," Boxer answered.

Edwardo spoke to the driver; then he said to Boxer, "We are going into the city."

Boxer nodded. He was tempted to ask where, but decided it would go down better if he didn't. For the same reason, he didn't ask any questions about their boss, Sanchez.

"I hope you like Spanish food," Miguel said.

"Very much," Boxer answered, "especially shrimps with salsa verde."

Pleased with his answer, the two men laughed.

Boxer and his two companions had a leisurely dinner which ended with delicious flan. By the time they finally left the restaurant, it was ten o'clock.

As soon as they were outside, Boxer looked for the limo. It had been parked across the street. But now a gray Buick was there.

"That's our car," Miguel said.

Boxer didn't ask any questions about the switch.

"I'll drive," Edwardo said, opening the door on the driver's side.

"You sit up front," Miguel told Boxer.

As soon as the three of them were settled in the car, Edwardo fished a large keyring from his pocket and tried three different keys in the ignition before he found one that worked.

"On a job like this," Edwardo explained, "you always use someone else's car. When we're done, we'll meet up with the limo again. Look behind us and you'll see it."

Boxer turned. The limo was behind them.

They returned to Brooklyn via the Manhattan Bridge and drove south along Flatbush Avenue.

"Now you tell us, Captain, what you want done," Miguel said, leaning forward from the rear seat.

"I've been thinking about it," Boxer said.

"Anything you want."

"I want to make sure they'll never mug another person," Boxer said.

"Kill them then," Edwardo suggested.

"What about the woman?" Miguel asked.

"No killing," Boxer said. "I don't want to kill them . . .I want them to remember every day of their lives what they did to my mother."

"They mugged your mother?" Miguel asked.

"They mugged and beat her," Boxer explained in a low, flat voice. "Then she went into a coma and died."

"And you don't want to kill them?" Edwardo said.

"I want them to suffer. You kill them and it's over. I want them to suffer for the rest of their miserable lives."

The two men nodded sympathetically and Edwardo said, "We will take care of them."

And Miguel added, "They will never forget."

Boxer accepted their comments silently. His thoughts moved back to the *Turtle* and his up-coming assignment. Both were unknown quantities. The *Turtle* was bound to have quirks, bugs—problems that should be understood and corrected before going out on a mission. And the mission itself was one of those that began with sealed orders. Boxer pursed his lips and ran his hand over his beard. All missions were unknown quantities until they were over. But . . .

"We are here," Edwardo said, pulling into an empty space and cutting the ignition, then the lights.

Boxer had been so involved with his own thoughts that he had no idea they had turned off Flatbush Avenue.

Each man fitted a silencer to the .357 he carried.

Boxer freed his snub nose .38 from its holster.

"Let's go amigos," Edwardo said.

The three of them left the car, and quickly crossed the street. Several men and women were sitting outside a large apartment house halfway up the street. They were drinking beer and a ghetto-blaster radio blared.

The three of them entered the small lobby.

"It stinks in here," Miguel said in a low voice.

Neither Boxer nor Edwardo commented.

Miguel took the lead. Boxer was behind him and Edwardo brought up the rear. The three of them started up the stairs. The stairway was dimly lit. On the third floor there wasn't any light at all.

"What the hell is that smell?" Boxer asked.

"Probably a mixture of garbage, dead rats and smell of tonight's cooking," Miguel whispered.

They reached the fourth floor.

Miguel reached into his pocket and took out two keys, inserted one into one lock and the other into the second lock. He motioned to Edwardo to turn the top one.

Edwardo eased the key slowly to the right.

"Captain," Miguel whispered.

Boxer slowly turned the key in the second lock.

Miguel nodded.

Edwardo touched Boxer on the arm and said, "You follow us." Then he stepped in front of him.

"Ready?" whispered Miguel.

Edwardo answered in Spanish.

Boxer suddenly realized his heart was thumping and his mouth was very dry.

Miguel put his hand on the door knob and carefully turned it.

Boxer could see the beads of sweat on Miguel's and Edwardo's foreheads—and on his own.

Miguel put his weight against the door.

Boxer's heart was pounding.

The door opened.

Miguel entered the apartment, Edwardo went in and Boxer followed.

Miguel pointed directly ahead of them to a cot in the living room and then motioned to the back of the apartment. "The man and woman are in the big bedroom and the other is in the small room."

"I'll hold this one here until you get the others," Boxer heard himself say. His voice was dry and hard.

Miguel nodded and motioned to Edwardo.

Boxer moved toward the cot. In a matter of moments he was standing over the man. Slowly he moved the revolver close to the front of the man's head. Then he pressed the muzzle hard against the man's forehead.

The man's eyes sprung open.

Boxer clamped his free hand over the man's mouth. "Get up slowly," Boxer told him, "or you're a dead man."

The man sat up.

Out of the corner of his eye, Boxer saw Miguel moving a man in front of him.

Then suddenly a woman screamed.

"Shut the fuck up!" Edwardo barked. "The two of you into the living room."

"I'm naked," the woman said.

"More than one guy has seen your cunt," Edwardo answered. "Now move." He herded them into the living room. "That's all of them," he said to Boxer.

"Turn the light on," Boxer said.

The ceiling light came on.

"We ain't got no money, man," the man who had been in bed with the woman said.

"I got an ounce of—"

"Cut the shit," Boxer snapped. "I'll make it short and sweet. A few months back you three pieces of shit beat up on an old woman. The woman died . . . and I'm

117

her son."

"Holy Christ!" one of the men exclaimed and made the mistake of moving.

Miguel slammed him across the chest with the .357.

The man staggered and gasped for air.

"No one move!" Miguel said flatly.

"Listen," the man who was on the cot said, "it was a mistake. We didn't mean—"

"It was the biggest mistake of your lives," Boxer said.

"I have a deal for you," the man who had come out of the small room said. "See the bitch there. . . . Each of you can have her. . . . She'll do whatever you want."

The woman nodded. "Hey, I'll even take two of you on at the same time, if that's what you want."

"No deals," Boxer said.

"What the fuck are you going to do?" the same man asked.

"The three men over there on the couch," Boxer said.

The men hesitated.

"Move," Miguel said. "Move, or I'll shove this barrel up your ass and pull the trigger."

The three men sat down.

"You slime balls are never going to forget this night," Boxer said. "You're never going to forget the old lady you beat up. But if you don't forget what we look like, you'll be dead within a week. Do you understand?"

The three men nodded.

"Not good enough," Boxer said. "I want to hear it out loud."

One by one they said what Boxer wanted them to say.

He turned to the woman. "You too," he said. "I want to hear it from you."

"I won't remember you," she answered.

Boxer nodded.

"Blow away one of their knee caps," Boxer said.

The three men started to stand.

118

There was a pop and one of the men dropped to the floor. Another pop sent the second man falling back on the couch. The third pop dropped the man to the floor.

The woman was too frightened to scream. Her mouth was open but no sound came out.

"Let's get out of here," Boxer said.

Miguel opened the door. The three of them left the apartment, hurried down the steps and out of the building.

"Everyone accounted for," Edwardo said, as soon as he put the car in motion.

"Everyone," Boxer said, his heart still racing.

"We'll meet the limo at Church and Flatbush," he said. "Then it's to the airport and back to Washington."

"Back to Washington," Boxer echoed. He suddenly felt drained. But knew he wouldn't close his eyes until they were airborne.

Ten

For a few moments Boxer stood over Trish. She was asleep. Her long blond hair cascaded over the pillow. One breast was bare. She was lovely to look at. He bent over her and gently kissed her lips.

She opened her eyes.

"Hello," Boxer said, caressing her bare breast.

"I'm glad you're back," she said. "I was having bad dreams . . . What time is it?"

Boxer looked at the red numbers on the digital clock. "Three," he told her.

"Call my grandfather," she said, "and call Stark. The two of them have been trying to get you all night." She reached up to a reading lamp and turned it on.

"It's three—"

"Call them. They said it was important."

Boxer picked up the phone and dialed Kinkade's private number.

After one ring, Kinkade answered.

"Boxer here."

"Captain Rugger's body and the bodies of four other ship's officers were washed ashore at Cape May, New Jersey," Kinkade said. "All ID's have been made."

"Drowned?"

"Shot in the back of the head and thrown into the water," Kinkade said.

Boxer's jaw tightened.

"The medical examiner says the bodies have been in the water for at least five days," Kinkade said.

"That means it's almost certain that the *T* didn't go down," Boxer said.

"It's about as certain as it's going to be until we find her," Kinkade said.

"But who the hell would have—"

"We won't get into that now," Kinkade said.

"Rugger didn't have any family," Boxer said. "I'll stand funeral expenses for him and any other member of the *T*'s crew who doesn't have a family to claim the body."

"I'm having all of the files of the deceased checked," Kinkade said. "I'll let you know later today."

"Okay," Boxer answered and hung up.

Trish pushed herself up and rested against the back of the bed.

Boxer started to dial Stark's number.

"Want to tell me about it?" Trish asked, putting her hand over his to stop him from dialing. "I'm really a very good listener."

"Rugger's body and the bodies of several other men were washed ashore at Cape May," Boxer said.

"How terrible!" she exclaimed.

Boxer nodded.

"But how could that have happened?" Trish asked.

"I can't tell you anything more," Boxer said. He freed his hand from hers and continued to dial.

Stark answered on the first ring too.

"I just spoke to Kinkade," Boxer said. He knew that Stark would know who was speaking.

"More bodies will probably come ashore over the next few weeks," Stark said.

"Probably," Boxer answered.

"Any ideas about what is going on?"

"Kinkade thinks the Ruskies have the *T*," Boxer said.

121

"What do you think?" Stark asked.

"Kinkade could be right," Boxer said.

"But why would they want the *Tecumseh*?"

"I can't answer that," Boxer said.

"Neither can I," Stark replied.

"I'll take care of the funeral arrangements for Rugger and anyone whose body is not claimed."

"I have Rugger's will," Stark said. "Be in my office at eleven hundred hours this morning and we'll go over it together. Rugger's lawyer will join us."

Boxer put his hand over the mouthpiece and said to Trish, "I have to be in Stark's office at eleven this morning."

"Don't see that you have much choice," she answered.

Boxer removed his hand from the phone's mouthpiece. "See you at eleven, Admiral."

"See you," Stark answered and hung up.

Boxer put the phone down. "I'm very tired," he said. "I'm going to shower and hopefully get a few hours sleep."

Trish got out of bed and followed him to the bathroom. "Are we going to get away for a couple of days?" she asked.

"We'll leave as soon as I'm finished with Stark and Rugger's lawyer," Boxer explained as he undressed. "Stark has Rugger's will and he wants to go over it."

"I'll pack and meet you with the car in front of—"

"Fine," Boxer said, stepping into the shower, "We'll do whatever you want."

"Until something else—" She stopped when she heard the sound of the water and padded back to the bed.

Boxer enjoyed the hot water pouring over him. He closed his eyes and tilted his face up toward the shower head. Rugger's death upset him, more than he was willing to show Trish. He genuinely liked the man.

Trish was sitting up when Boxer returned to the

122

bedroom. "I was thinking that we might go to western Maryland or maybe to the Blue Ridge Mountains," she said.

"Anywhere you want to go will be fine with me," he answered, climbing into bed. He reached up and switched off the reading lamp.

Trish eased down and pressed close to Boxer. "Hold me."

He put his arm around her waist.

"Where did you go with those two men?" Trish asked.

"To New York," he answered, feeling himself sink into the gray haze that precedes sleep.

"Why?"

Boxer shook his head.

"Jack, you can't expect me to—"

He opened his eyes. "You don't have to know about certain things. Now please, let me sleep."

Trish sat up.

"What's wrong?" Boxer asked.

"I just can't do it," she said.

Boxer sat up. "Okay, tell me what you can't do?"

"If I had gone off with two women the way you went off with those two men, wouldn't you want to know why?"

"Why?" he repeated. "I'll tell you why. But I don't want to discuss it. I don't want to know what you think about it and you're never to tell another person. Agreed?"

"Agreed," she answered in a high pitched voice.

"I went to kill the men who beat my mother into a coma," he said.

"Did you?"

"Go to sleep!"

"Did you kill them?"

"No," Boxer answered. "I did worse—I had them crippled for life. Now go to sleep." He settled down on

123

his back and closed his eyes.

"You really did that?" Trish asked, moving close to him again.

"The two men with me kneecapped them," Boxer said. "But I ordered it done."

After a few moments of silence, Trish asked, "Are you asleep?"

"Almost," Boxer answered.

"Hold me," she said.

Boxer put his hand on her breast, but she moved it between her thighs.

A pert lieutenant with long black hair and soft black eyes was at the desk outside Stark's office where Cynthia should have been.

"Captain Boxer," Boxer said, "to see Admiral Stark."

"The Admiral is expecting you," she said. She spoke with a decided western twang.

Boxer nodded, went to the door and knocked.

"Come," Stark called.

Boxer entered the office and closed the door behind him.

Stark was at his desk. "Two bodies came ashore at Virginia Beach just two hours ago. They're being examined now."

Boxer crossed the room and without an invitation, he sat down in the chair on Stark's right.

"Forty men crewed the *Tecumseh*," Stark said in his gravelly voice.

"Sharks probably got some of them," Boxer commented.

Stark took a cigar from the humidor. "Care for one?" he asked.

"Why not," Boxer answered.

Stark handed him the cigar he was holding and took

another for himself. "Don't fucking well like what's happening," he said, after he lit up.

"What are you going to do if it turns out to be the Ruskies?" Boxer asked.

"The President and his advisors will decide that," Stark answered.

The phone rang.

Stark picked it up and listened for a moment; then he said, "Send him in. Rugger's lawyer is here . . . name is Wheeler, Francine Wheeler."

"That's a very pretty woman manning the desk outside," Boxer commented.

Stark smiled. "She's temporary. Commander Lowe will be back there when she returns. I gave her a few days for herself before the mission."

"You certainly have an eye for—"

A soft knock at the door stopped Boxer from completing the sentence.

Stark called out, "Come!"

The door opened and a statuesque red headed woman entered the office. She wore a light tan summer dress and tan shoes. She carried a brown leather attache case.

Boxer followed Stark's lead and stood up.

Stark reached across the desk, shook Wheeler's hand and introduced her to Boxer.

"A pleasure to meet you," Wheeler said. "Bill had, as you see, the highest regard for you."

"I had a great deal of regard for him too," Boxer answered, unable to place her accent.

As soon as all of them were seated, Wheeler said, "I'll get right to the heart of the situation. According to the deceased's will, Captain Boxer inherits the entire estate."

"What?" Boxer started out of his chair; then stopped his movement and sat down again.

"Everything," Wheeler said.

"What does 'everything' mean?" Boxer asked.

125

"His house, his paintings, his automobile, his art collection—"

"Art collection?" Boxer questioned.

Wheeler nodded. "He paid about a half million dollars for it over a period of twenty five years, but the current market value will probably be three times that. Captain Boxer, in round figures, you have been willed between four and five million dollars."

This time Boxer launched himself out of the chair. "Are you sure there isn't anyone—"

"The will is iron clad . . . I drew it up for him, but—"

"But what?"

"There is a natural son."

"Where?"

"Staten Island, New York. He lives with an aunt. The mother abandoned the child."

"How old is he?"

"Seventeen."

"What's his name?" Boxer asked.

"Charles Spadaro. Spadaro was the mother's last name."

"How do you know about him?"

"Bill set up a special fund. I send money to the aunt for the boy every month."

"Give me the boy's address and—"

"Are you sure you want to start something that might turn out to be a real can of worms?" Wheeler asked.

"I'm not sure of anything," Boxer said, "except that I don't need Bill's money."

"Would you like me to probate the will?" Wheeler asked.

"Yes."

Wheeler nodded. "Admiral Stark is the only executor."

"Then you knew about this?" Boxer asked.

Stark shook his head. "Bill asked me if I would be his executor and I said yes. He also told me to contact

126

Wheeler if something should happen to him."

"Is there anything else you would like to know about the estate, Captain?" Wheeler asked.

"Nothing at this time," Boxer answered. "But I want that address now."

Stark gave Wheeler a piece of note paper.

"Twenty-one Beach Street," Wheeler said, handing Boxer the piece of paper.

"Do you know anything about the boy?" Boxer asked, pocketing the piece of paper.

Wheeler shrugged. "He's been in trouble with the cops a few times."

"Does he know Bill is his father?"

"I'm not sure," Wheeler answered. "I know that Bill saw the boy a couple of times a year."

"Does the aunt have a phone?" Boxer asked.

"An unlisted number," Wheeler answered.

"That's no problem," Boxer said, looking at Stark to confirm what he had just said.

"None," Stark responded with a nod.

"Is there anything else I should know?" Boxer asked.

"Nothing," Wheeler said.

"Good. You probate the will, and I'm going to make a quick trip to Staten Island to see the boy."

"When?" Stark asked.

"Today. I want to see the boy before—"

Stark cut him short. "I understand."

"Here's my card," Wheeler said. "During the normal business day you can always reach me at the office. Other times you might try my home number. If I'm not there, the housekeeper will know where I can be reached."

Boxer thanked her.

Wheeler stood up and shook Boxer's hand. "It's been a pleasure to meet you, Captain. A real pleasure." She turned to Stark. "Thank you, Admiral, for giving the time."

"My pleasure," Stark said, standing.

The two of them shook hands and Boxer escorted Wheeler to the door.

"There is one thing I would like to discuss with you when you have time," Wheeler said.

"Oh?"

"It concerns one of Bill's paintings . . . Perhaps we might be able to do it over drinks."

Boxer nodded. He was certain that she had posed nude for Bill. "I will be away for two to three weeks. When I return, we'll have drinks and discuss the painting."

"Thank you," she said. "And good luck with the boy."

"Thanks. Let's hope I don't need too much luck and that—"

"I don't believe in miracles," Wheeler commented.

"Unfortunately neither do I," Boxer said, aware of the scent of the woman's perfume. "But maybe this time it'll happen."

Wheeler nodded. "Maybe." Then she left the office.

Boxer closed the door and returned to the chair. "Might have told me that the lawyer was a woman," Boxer said.

"Her name should have done that," Stark answered.

"I guess it didn't register," Boxer said; then he asked, "Do you think I might be able to use government transportation. I promised to spend the remaining time ashore with Trish. But now I have the boy to see."

"I'll arrange for you to be 'Coptered to New York, and a limo will take you from the base to the boy's home. A 'Copter will take you to the *Turtle*."

"That'll be fine," Boxer responded.

"You know," Stark said, "Wheeler might be right about becoming involved with the boy. It could very well become a can of worms."

Boxer shrugged. "I'll have to take my chances. If it turns out to be a can of worms, then at least I'll have tried to give the boy a chance to become something more than he now could. If it works, I will have done something worthwhile for another human being."

"You know," Stark said, "despite what you do, you're really a very caring man."

Boxer shrugged. "Maybe the boy is worth caring about. Besides, as far as I'm concerned, I don't have any other way to go."

"This is Beach Street, Captain," the limo's driver said, as they turned into a street with rundown one and two family houses on either side. There wasn't a driveway that didn't have a battered car in it and some had two. Garbage was strewn all over and most lawns were overgrown with weeds, though here and there Boxer saw a forlorn bush of roses.

"Twenty-One is on the right side," Trish said. "There, that white house. My God it looks worse than most of them."

"Pull up," Boxer told the driver. "I want you to wait outside the car."

"Aye, aye sir. But we'd be better off with a couple of more men. The neighbors already have their eyes poppin' out of their heads," the driver said, stopping the car and turning off the ignition. He left his place behind the wheel and opened the door for Boxer and Trish.

"I feel as if there are hundreds of pairs of eyes looking at me," Trish said, as they walked toward the house.

"There are," Boxer answered, taking hold of her arm.

Suddenly a group of four teenaged boys emerged from around the right side of the house.

Trish faltered.

"Keep walking," Boxer said, speaking from between his teeth. The boys were bare chested. All of them wore a red head band and each of them had several gold chains around his neck. They were tan, muscular and looked

129

menacing. Boxer tried to match each of their faces to Rugger's. But he couldn't find a resemblance.

"Wha' ya want?" one of them asked.

"I'm looking for someone," Boxer said, slowing his pace.

"You a cop?" another one of the boys asked.

"No."

"Den why ya lookin' for someone?" the first boy asked.

"I'm looking for Ch—" Boxer was going to say Charles, but instead he said, "I'm looking for Chuck Spadaro."

The boys moved and blocked his way to the two steps leading to the front door.

"Why don't ya take that nice piece of ass, turn around an' go away before youse gets hurt," a third boy said.

Boxer was close to him. "What did you say?" he asked, stalling for time.

"Dis guy is deaf," the boy laughed. "I told ya to—"

Boxer's right hand leaped out. He grabbed hold of the boy between his neck and right shoulder.

"Shit!" the boy exclaimed, struggling to get free. "Shit!"

Boxer forced him to his knees. "You're very sorry for what you said, isn't that right?"

"Yes . . . Yes."

"Say it," Boxer said, gripping the boy harder and harder.

"I'm very sorry for what I said," the boy whimpered.

Boxer pushed him off to one side and let go of him. He looked over his shoulder. A few of the adult males were coming toward the house. "This is a family matter," Boxer said loud enough for them to hear. "Now you punks move aside and let us enter."

A frowsy looking woman in a house coat stuck her

head out of an upstairs window. "What's goin' on?" she shouted.

"Captain Rugger sent me," Boxer called out.

She shouted something in Italian and the boys moved away; then she said, "Chuck come inside."

"I don't want to," answered the first boy who spoke to Boxer.

"This man comes from Uncle Bill," the woman said.

"Better come inside," Boxer said, "or I'll carry you in."

"Yeah, you an' what army?" Chuck challenged.

Boxer went toward him. "I don't have time to fuck with a punk like you," he said. "Either you get your ass in that house, or I'll beat the shit out of you in front of your friends. And if you don't think I can do it, try me."

Chuck looked at Trish.

"He can and will," she said.

"Alright . . . Alright, I'm going inside," Chuck said. He turned to his friends. "See you guys in a little while." And he went up the steps and opened the door.

Boxer and Trish followed him into a small foyer, through a dining room, with a large table, and into a musty smelling living room.

The woman came down the steps and following her was a heavy-set man wearing shorts, a tank top and blue sneakers without laces. "I'm Chuck's aunt," she said, introducing herself, "and that's my friend Vinny."

Boxer and Trish shook hands with Rose and Vinny.

Rose gestured to a couch covered with plastic. "Please sit down," she said. "I wasn't expectin' no company, or I'd have taken the cover off the couch."

"It's alright," Trish said. "We're sorry to have come without calling."

Rose nodded. "You people hungry?" she asked and before anyone could answer, she said, "Vinny go get a

131

pizza and a couple of six-packs of beer."

"I think I should stay and listen to what these people have to say," Vinny said.

"I'll go," Chuck said.

"I want you here," Boxer said.

"Then if nobody's going, I'll make coffee," Rose said.

"Mrs.—" Boxer began.

"Mrs. Caliendo," Rose said. "Caliendo is my married name, but I'm separated from my husband."

Boxer nodded and said, "Mrs. Caliendo, Captain Rugger died at sea."

"Oh my God!" she exclaimed, crossing herself. "God rest his soul."

"Does dat mean you don't get any more checks?" Vinny asked.

Boxer glared at him.

"What's wrong wid you?" Vinny asked. "Don't ya know it takes bread to feed and clothe a boy like Chuck? That kid has everything. Look at those gold chains he's wearing!"

"The checks will continue," Boxer said.

"Then what's the problem?" Vinny asked.

Boxer looked at Rose. He knew it wasn't the way to do it, but he didn't have the time to play games. "Does Chuck know who Bill really was?"

She started to speak, but changed her mind.

"Yeah, I know. Bill was my uncle. So big deal!"

"He was your father," Boxer said, snapping out the words. "So that's the big deal, punk. Captain Rugger was your father."

Chuck's jaw went slack; he looked at his aunt. "No shit?" he asked.

"Bill was your father," Rose answered.

Chuck began to pace up and down the living room. Suddenly he stopped. "So why lay that on me now?" he asked, looking at Boxer.

132

"Why indeed?" Boxer asked disgustedly.

"What's that supposed to mean?" Vinny questioned.

"I'll put it to you this way, Chuck. Bill was a very good friend of mine."

"So?"

"So when he died," Boxer said, "he left me between four and five million dollars."

"You jerkin' us off?" Vinny asked.

Boxer pointed his finger at him. "One more comment from you and you're going to have my fist in your mouth . . . You understand."

"Hey, you think you're so fuckin' tough," Vinny said, starting out of the chair.

"Vinny, don't make a fool of yourself," Boxer said calmly. "Just sit there and keep your mouth shut."

"Who are you?" Chuck asked.

"A very good friend of your father. Now listen to me. I have to go away for several weeks. When I come back, I'm going to come here again. Between then and now, you have a lot of hard thinking to do. You have to decide whether you want that four or five million—"

"Sure I want it," Chuck said.

"Good. Then you don't have to think about that . . . But think about this: I'm the only guy who can give it to you. That's right: I'm the guy who can do it."

"What's the hitch?" Chuck asked.

Boxer was glad to see that Chuck wasn't as stupid as he appeared to be. "You get nothing without giving something."

"You swing both ways?" Chuck asked, looking at Trish.

"Listen," Boxer said, "and stop thinking with your cock. The only way you're ever going to see any of that money is earn it and the only way you're going to earn it, is to make something of yourself."

"You mean like going to school . . . college . . . shit

133

like that?"

"That's exactly what I mean. You'll have a few weeks to think about it," Boxer said getting to his feet and motioning Trish to stand.

"So now what?" Vinny asked.

"Now I go and you do some thinking," Boxer said.

"What about her," Vinny asked.

"Nothing about her," Boxer said. "No matter what Chuck decides she'll continue to receive the check."

"But now we're talking four or five million. Part of that belongs to her," Vinny said.

"All of it belongs to me," Boxer answered. "If you don't believe me, hire a lawyer and let him tell you."

"Rose, I'll call my friend Doug," Vinny said.

"I'll be back in a few weeks," Boxer told Chuck. "You've got a lot of thinking to do."

"Can't I call you?"

"No," Boxer answered. He took hold of Trish's arm and steered her to the door.

Chuck, Rose and Vinny followed them.

"That's a government limo," Vinny said. "Who the hell are you?"

Boxer smiled. "Don't try to guess."

"Shit, Vinny," Chuck said, "It's none of your fuckin' business who he is."

"Better listen to the kid," Boxer advised.

Boxer and Trish wound up remaining in New York. They booked into the Park Central and took a two room suite that overlooked Central Park from the thirtieth floor.

As soon as Boxer tipped the bellboy and he and Trish were alone, he took her in his arms. "I know you wanted to be in the country," he said. "But—"

"I want to be with you," she said. "I want to be where-

134

ever you are."

Boxer slid his hands down her back and taking hold of her buttocks, he pressed her to him. "I'm going to miss you, Trish," he said.

"Love me," she whispered passionately.

Boxer kissed her lips.

She opened her mouth and gave him her tongue.

Boxer ran his hands over her rump.

"I'm not wearing all that much," she told him.

"I want you naked," Boxer answered, letting go of her.

She stepped away from him, undid the buttons down the front of her dress and slipped it off. "See, just a thin bra and a pair of briefs."

"Take them off," Boxer commanded.

She reached around to her back and undoing the hooks of the bra, she let it fall to the floor. "You do the briefs," she told him.

Boxer started toward her.

"You strip first," Trish said.

Boxer took off his shirt and tossed it on a chair. He kicked off the loafers he was wearing, then took off his pants and laid them over the chair. His T-shirt followed, then his shorts. "This okay?" he asked.

She pointed to his socks. "Those go too."

"Gone," he said, pulling off his socks.

Trish came to him. "Now strip me!"

Wrapping his arms around her, Boxer kissed the right side of her neck; then moving slightly away, he pressed his face between her bare breasts. They were warm, slightly moist and smelled slightly of musk.

"Suck my nipples," she said.

Boxer put his lips to one erect bud and then the other, while she delicately teased the head of his shaft.

"I can feel its heat," she whispered.

"Your whole body is warm."

"Inside I'm on fire," she told him.

135

Boxer slowly sank to his knees and burying his face in the hollow of her stomach, he moved her pink, flimsy, briefs down her thighs and legs until they were at her feet.

"You know what I want," Trish said, caressing his hair.

"Patience," Boxer answered, looking up at her. He raised his hands and placing the palms of his hands under her breasts, he spread his fingers over them.

"I'm not good at being patient," she breathed.

"And I'm not good when I'm rushed," Boxer answered with a grin. "Good things happen slowly."

"What good things?" she asked, putting her hands over his and squeezing them.

"Things like this," Boxer said, slipping his hands away from hers and taking hold of the cheeks of her rump. "And this," he added, placing his lips on the warm, moist vagina.

Trish trembled, sucked in her breath and made a low, wordless sound of pleasure when she exhaled.

"Hey, maybe this is too much for you?" Boxer teased.

"Never," she answered, pressing him hard against her vagina. "From you it's never enough."

Boxer moved his face away from her body. "It's time to make use of the bed," he said, standing.

"In a minute," Trish answered, sinking to her knees in front of him and taking his penis into her mouth.

A delicious wave of pleasure flowed from her warm lips into his body. He closed his eyes, while she used her tongue on him.

"Am I good?" she questioned.

Boxer opened his eyes and looked down at her. "On a scale of one to ten, I'd say you were nine and a half."

"Bastard!"

"Do it again and I'll see if you can make ten," Boxer said.

136

"Listen," she said, standing up, "if you can't appreciate talent, there are many men who can."

Boxer scooped her up in his arms and dropped her on the bed. "I'll put one of those chastity belts on you."

Trish began to laugh.

"What's so funny?" Boxer asked, caressing her wet vagina.

"I had this crazy vision of a woman wearing one of those things and her lover trying to get through it," she said, gently moving her hand over his shaft.

"It would be difficult," Boxer said.

"Very," she said, her voice suddenly tight.

"I love you, Trish," Boxer told her.

"And I love you," she answered. "I loved you even before we made love. I know that sounds crazy, but it's true . . . and now I couldn't ever let another man touch me."

"No other man ever will," Boxer said.

Trish splayed her thighs. "Come into me, my darling."

Boxer entered her and immediately began to move.

Trish thrust herself against him. "See," she said, "I'm no good at all when it comes to waiting . . . I'm coming, my love . . . I'm coming. . . ."

"So am I!" Boxer exclaimed, his body shuddering from orgasmic ecstasy. . . .

After several moments passed, Trish uttered a deep sigh and then she said, "Now tell me that wasn't a ten?"

"That was a ten," Boxer said, kissing the tip of her nose. "That was even a twelve."

"But the scale only goes to ten," Trish said.

"That scale was for sucking; this is for fucking and for fucking you rate a twelve," Boxer said. "It was absolutely a twelve. . . ."

Eleven

Boxer, Bush and Cowly were on the secondary bridge.

"All hands aboard, Skipper," Cowly said, putting the phone down.

Boxer pointed to the northeast. "Will you look at that lightning!"

Within moments a boom of thunder crashed around them.

"The rain is going to come before we clear the bay," Bush said.

"Sheets of it," Boxer commented, as another streak of lightning made a white jagged line between the earth and the rapidly moving clouds.

"That was damn close," Cowly said.

Thunder exploded.

"I could feel that," Bush said.

Boxer switched on the MC and two high intensity searchlights. "Deck detail," he said, "stand by to cast off."

"Forward detail, detail standing by," the mate in charge reported.

"Aft detail, standing by," the second chief said.

Boxer looked at Cowly. "Check all major systems."

Cowly changed the positions of two switches and looked down at the SYSCOPE. "Systems normal," he reported.

"Cast off forward line," Boxer said.

"Forward line off," the mate reported.

"Cast off stern line," Boxer ordered.

"Stern line off," the chief reported.

Boxer keyed the EO. "Reverse engines, fourteen hundred rpms."

"Reverse engines, fourteen hundred rpms," the EO repeated.

"Mahony," Boxer said, speaking to the helmsman, "hold her steady."

"Steady as she goes, Skipper," Mahony answered.

Boxer scanned the sky again. "I'd like to be in the channel before the rain comes."

The Radar Officer keyed Boxer. "Skipper, what's the critical distance between us and any other craft?"

"Keep it at five thousand yards," Boxer answered.

"Roger that," the RO answered.

"Helmsman, come to course zero four degrees," Boxer said.

"Coming to course zero four degrees," Mahony answered.

The *Turtle*'s stern began to swing to the port side.

Boxer keyed the EO. "Stop all engines . . . Stand by."

"Aye, aye, Skipper . . . Stopping all engines . . . Standing by," the EO responded.

The *Turtle* continued to drop off to the port side.

"Zero five knots," Boxer said.

"Zero five knots," the EO answered.

"Helmsman," Boxer said, "come to course eight four degrees."

"Coming to course eight four degrees," Mahony answered.

The *Turtle* began to slide forward and turn into the main channel.

Boxer switched off the search lights.

"Cowly, Bush, take the INFRASCOPE," Boxer said.

Bush turned on the portside instrument and Cowly did the same with the device on the starboard.

"The radar sometimes misses the small craft," Boxer explained. "I don't want to run over anyone and then go back and pick up the pieces."

The lightning had moved off to the southwest, but the air was heavy with moisture.

The Communications Officer keyed Boxer. He was one of the new men aboard. "Sir, a new weather advisory has just come from the National Weather Service."

"Read it," Boxer said.

"'Severe thunder showers for the entire Chesapeake Bay area, with strong winds and gusts up to five zero knots.' Then there's a warning to aircraft about wind sheer conditions at the various airports in the area."

"Roger that," Boxer said, noting that the wind had picked up and it had gotten perceptibly cooler. He turned to Cowly. "I could use a jacket, what about you?"

"Not a bad idea," Cowly answered.

"You want your jacket too?" Boxer asked, turning his attention to Bush.

Before Bush could answer, the RO keyed Boxer, "Skipper, airborne target . . . Two four zero degrees . . . Altitude fifteen thousand feet—"

"Only surface targets," Boxer said.

"Skipper, this plane is jumping all over the sky," the RO said.

"Range?" Boxer asked.

"Twelve thousand yards . . . Holy Christ, she's dropping!"

"What?"

"She's coming down," RO answered.

The COMMO keyed Boxer. "Sir, we've got a May Day coming in from an aircraft."

Boxer switched on the MC. "All hands now hear this . . . Now hear this . . . We're responding to a May

140

Day . . . All hands now hear this . . . We're responding to a May Day . . . Mister Vargas report to the bridge."

Boxer switched off the MC. "Helmsman, come to course two four degrees."

"Coming to course two four degrees," Mahony answered.

Boxer keyed the EO. "One five knots," he said.

"Going to one five knots," the EO reported.

Vargas came on to the bridge.

"Spic, get a half dozen men in the water when we come to a stop and four inflatables. Have the rest of your team on deck and ready with blankets, hot coffee and tea."

"Got it, Skipper," Vargas answered.

Boxer nodded and keyed COMMO. "Anything else on the plane?" he asked.

"It's Central Flight two five zero out of Fort Wayne and going to Norfolk," the COMMO said.

"Roger that," Boxer said.

The RO keyed Boxer. "Target just left the scope."

"Roger that," Boxer said; then he keyed COMMO. "On all frequencies except those used for code ten situations, transmit the following message: the USN-Sixty-Nine responding to May Day . . . Will need additional assistance."

"Aye, aye, Skipper."

"Keep sending until we reach the crash sight," Boxer said.

"Aye, aye."

Boxer turned to Bush. "I didn't plan this." he said.

"I believe you," Bush answered. "But it certainly has all your earmarks."

"I bet Kinkade will say the same thing when he hears about it," Boxer commented.

"You can be sure of it," Bush said.

Boxer nodded. His preliminary orders were to head straight out to sea.

The COMMO keyed Boxer. "Skipper, I have Coasty on the radio who wants to speak to you."

"Patch him through," Boxer responded.

"Go ahead, Skipper," the COMMO said.

"This is Captain Boxer."

"This is Commander Williams of the United States Coast Guard . . . Who the hell are you? What the hell are you doing out there?"

Boxer smiled. "Commander we'll be at the crash sight in five minutes . . . Have your boats meet us there."

"I can't ID your ship number," Williams said.

"Never mind Commander . . . Just get your ships there . . . Out," Boxer said.

"Skipper," COMMO said, keying him again, "Headquarters is on the radio."

"Tell them I'm too busy to speak to them now. I'll get back to them later."

"Aye, aye, Skipper," the COMMO said.

"Kinkade is going to love that," Bush commented.

"Love it or not," Boxer said, "he's going to have to live with it."

"Skipper," the COMMO said, "there's another advisory from the National Weather Service."

"Better or worse?"

"Worse."

"I'll stay with the one you already gave me," Boxer said.

"Ten four," the COMMO answered.

Suddenly a gust of wind slammed into the *Turtle* from the portside and she rolled ten degrees to the starboard.

"That really came out of nowhere," Boxer commented.

The RO keyed Boxer. "Skipper, very heavy rain coming at us from northeast."

"Roger that," Boxer said.

"Cowly, Bush, see if you can spot the wreckage yet,"

142

Boxer said. "It'll be a lot easier before the rain comes."

The wind suddenly picked up and the chop in the bay changed to two to three foot waves.

"Can't see anything yet," Cowly reported.

"Negative," Bush said.

Suddenly a few drops of rain fell and then the wind-blown deluge swept over the *Turtle*.

"Stowe the INFRASCOPES," Boxer shouted above the howl of the wind.

The *Turtle* rolled violently.

Boxer wiped the rain out of his eyes and increased the intensity of the searchlights. But their beams were trapped by the wall of falling water.

Boxer keyed the EO. "Reduce speed to zero three knots."

"Reducing speed to zero three knots," the EO answered.

Boxer switched on the MC. "Vargas, get a couple of your men forward . . . Maybe they'll be able to spot something."

Vargas waved.

"If the wind would drop off," Bush said, "maybe we'd be able to hear them."

"We could pass the survivors and not even know it," Cowly said.

Boxer keyed the EO. "Stop all engines."

"Stopping all engines," the EO reported.

"Vargas," Boxer said over the MC, "launch your inflatables . . . Have them search around . . . Tell them to key in on our radio signal."

Again Vargas waved.

Boxer watched the inflatables slide off the *Turtle* deck and quickly vanish behind a curtain of water.

"Skipper," Cowly said, "we're rolling between three and five degrees."

"Can you get a read of the wind's speed?"

"Somewhere around twenty-five knots," Cowly answered.

"I sure as hell wouldn't want to be aboard in a real blow," Boxer commented.

The RO keyed Boxer. "Target approaching outer limit . . . Bearing four five degrees . . . Range fifty-five hundred yards . . . Speed one two knots."

"ID," Boxer said.

"The tanker, *Silver Star*."

"Roger that," Boxer answered; then he keyed the COMMO. "Signal the tanker *Silver Star* to slow down and come to our assistance."

"Aye, aye, sir," the COMMO answered.

Suddenly one of Vargas's men shot up a flare.

"On the port side!" Boxer exclaimed. "Get a fix on it."

Bush was at the Range Finder.

Another flare bloomed in the blackness.

"Got it!" Bush said. "One five zero yards."

Boxer keyed the EO. "Give me sufficient rpms to move one five zero yards.

"Eight hundred rpms for three five seconds. Say when."

"Stand by," Boxer said.

"Standing by," the EO answered.

Another flare went up.

"Three four degrees," Bush said.

"Mahony," Boxer said, "ease her over to three four degrees."

"Going to three four degrees," Mahony said.

Boxer keyed the EO. "Now!" he ordered, activating the digital stop clock on the COMCOMP.

"Eight hundred rpms," the EO said.

The *Turtle* shuddered and began to slide through the water.

Boxer checked the clock. He started counting aloud when the read-out reached twenty-five seconds.

The EO keyed him. "Thirty seconds, Skipper."

"Roger that," Boxer answered.

"Thirty-five seconds . . . All engines stopped," the EO said.

"Roger that," Boxer answered.

He looked down at the deck where Vargas's men were leaping into the water.

"Wreckage zero three points off port bow," Bush called out. "Wreckage zero three points off port bow!"

Boxer looked, straining his eyes to see through the heavy rain.

Suddenly one of the men on deck shouted. "There's one of our rafts . . . Hey, over this way!"

Out of the rain emerged an inflatable with survivors.

Boxer switched on the MC. "Get those people aboard!" he ordered.

"Starboard side," Cowly said, "raft off our starboard side."

The inflatable bumped against the *Turtle*.

The COMMO keyed Boxer. "Skipper, the *Silver Star* will assist."

"Roger that," Boxer said. "Tell her to come to full stop within two hundred yards of us."

"Aye, aye, Skipper," the COMMO said.

Boxer turned his attention to the deck. Some of the men in the water were helping people aboard.

The RO keyed Boxer. "Two targets heading this way . . . bearing two four degrees . . . Range forty-five hundred yards . . . Speed one eight knots."

"Roger that," Boxer said. He guessed they were Coastys.

"ID the Coast Guard cutters *Deep Sea* and *Wild River*," the RO said.

"Roger that," Boxer answered.

A third raft brought survivors to the *Turtle*.

"Skipper," the COMMO said, "the *Silver Star* is lying

off our port side . . . She has lowered two boats and has begun to search."

"Roger that," Boxer answered, watching the activity on the deck. Vargas's men worked efficiently, even though some of them were new.

The Medical Officer keyed Boxer. "Skipper, some of the survivors have been badly hurt and will require surgery."

"Any emergencies?"

"A pregnant woman . . . She has gone into labor . . . She's in her eighth month."

"Can you handle it?"

"I haven't delivered a baby since I was a resident, and that was almost twenty years ago."

"Can you handle it?"

"If it's routine, yes . . . but if it becomes complicated—"

"Go for the routine," Boxer answered.

"I'll sure as hell go for it," the MO answered.

"What about the others?"

"They can wait until they reach the hospital," the MO said.

"Keep me posted about the woman," Boxer said.

"Ten four," the MO answered.

"One of the women brought aboard has gone into labor," Boxer announced to Bush and Cowly.

"Interesting," Bush commented.

Cowly nodded. "The woman must be frightened out of her skull," he said.

Boxer agreed.

"Skipper," the RO said, "the *Silver Star* is closing with us."

Boxer switched on the MC. "Ahoy, *Silver Star* you're drifting toward us."

An instant later the deep vibrating sound of a ship's engines came out of the darkness.

146

"She won't be able to hold any position very long in this kind of sea," Cowly said.

Suddenly several search lights played over the *Turtle*.

"That must be our Coasty friends," Boxer said. He switched on the MC again. "Glad to see you guys," Boxer said.

"Have you picked up all the survivors?" one of the cutter captains asked over his MC.

"Haven't taken a head count yet," Boxer answered. "And there might be a few aboard the tanker, the *Silver Star* . . . She's assisting in the rescue."

"Stand by for further instructions," the cutter captain said.

Boxer looked at Cowly and at Bush; then the three of them started to laugh.

The COMMO keyed Boxer. "Skipper, Captain Williams is on the radio."

"Patch him in," Boxer said.

"Captain Boxer, you are to remain on station until—"

"Captain, the moment the weather moderates all survivors will be transferred to the cutters," Boxer said.

"In this situation my orders supersede all others," Williams said.

"Have your men on the cutters ready to take on survivors when the weather moderates," Boxer said, "or I will take them with me."

"But you can't do that!"

"I can't, but I will," Boxer said. "Do you read me?"

"I read you, Captain."

"Ten four," Boxer answered.

Despite the efforts of Vargas's men, only two more survivors were found and when dawn finally came, the broken bodies of four more people were found and taken aboard.

The wind and the rain continued, making the gray forms of the *Silver Star* and the two cutters barely visible.

147

Vargas came up to the bridge. "We got seventeen—five men and the rest women," he said. "Skipper, one of the women is Louise."

Boxer's jaw went slack.

"She's pregnant," Vargas said.

"I didn't know . . . the MO didn't tell me," Boxer answered. He and Louise had been lovers. He had planned to marry her and then for reasons completely unknown to him, she had sent him a "Dear John" letter and vanished so completely that at times he felt as if she had never existed. But he knew she did. She was the only black woman he had ever loved.

"She went into labor as soon as she was pulled out of the water," Vargas said.

"Bush, you have the CON," Boxer said.

"Aye, aye, Skipper," Bush answered.

Boxer left the bridge and hurried down into the sick bay. The MO was talking to one of the male survivors.

"Doc," Boxer called, "may I have a few words with you."

The MO excused himself and came over to Boxer.

"Why didn't you tell me who the pregnant woman was?" Boxer asked angrily.

"I thought you had enough to do on the bridge without giving you something more to think about."

"We'll discuss that later," Boxer said. "Right now, where is she?"

"I put her in the OR," the MO said.

Boxer nodded and walked toward the OR.

The MO went after him. "She's having a hard time of it . . . She's at the beginning of her eighth month."

Boxer stopped. "What's the bottom line?"

"She might need a cesarian section," the MO said.

"Can you do it?"

"If I had to, yes . . . but I'd prefer not to," he said. "Her husband is a doctor."

148

"How much time do you have before you'll know?" Boxer asked.

"An hour . . . two at the most."

"Better get your staff psyched-up to do a cesarian section," Boxer said and strode away. Once everything got back to normal he intended to have a long talk with the MO.

Boxer opened the door of the OR and entered the small, white room.

Louise was on a gurney, a white sheet covered her otherwise naked body.

"That you doctor?" she asked.

"No," Boxer said gently.

"Who is it?" she asked, trying to pull herself up in order to get a better look.

Boxer moved to her side. "It's me Louise, Jack."

"Oh my God!" she exclaimed, her hand going to her mouth.

"You'll be all right," he said, caressing the top of her head. "I promise you, you'll be all right."

She took hold of his free hand. "I . . . I . . ." Then she started to weep.

"There's no need for that," Boxer said gently.

"I'm married to—"

Boxer put his finger across her lips. "We'll talk after the baby comes," he told her. "Now you have to concentrate on yourself and the baby."

She put the back of his hand to her lips. "God help me," she whispered, "but when the pilot told us that we were going to crash in the bay, I prayed that you'd be close by . . . I knew if you were, you'd save me."

He bent down and kissed her forehead.

The COMMO keyed Boxer. "Skipper, Headquarters is kicking up a storm. Mister Kinkade wants to speak to you."

"Patch him through."

149

"What the fuck do you think you're doing?" Kinkade shrieked. "You're already behind schedule."

"Kinkade, I'll be where I'm supposed to be when I'm supposed to be there . . . Just keep yourself together."

"Don't tell me—"

"Out," Boxer said, switching off the radio.

"Bless you for taking the time to save us," Louise said.

"I'll be back in a little while," Boxer told her. "Try to rest."

"Jack," she said, "I married a good man."

Boxer nodded. "I'm glad you did . . . Now rest."

She squeezed his hand; then she let go.

As soon as Boxer left the OR, he went back to the MO. "You tell me what Louise needs, understand?"

"Aye, aye sir," the MO answered.

Boxer returned to the bridge. Neither the rain nor the wind had abated. But the daylight, though gray, made it easier to see the *Silver Star* and the two cutters.

"We're not going to be able to transfer the survivors to the cutters for several hours," Bush said. "I checked with the National Weather Service. The rain and wind won't let up until well into the afternoon."

Boxer nodded. "Kinkade is worried that we're behind schedule," he said.

"That man is always worried," Cowly commented.

"Always," Boxer agreed, "even when there's nothing to worry about."

"How is she?" Cowly asked. He liked Louise the first time he had met her.

"She might need a cesarian section," Boxer answered.

"Can the MO do it?"

Boxer nodded. "He's going to have to."

"Maybe," Cowly suggested, "Louise would be more comfortable if another woman was with her?"

"I never thought about that," Boxer said, switching

150

on the MC. "Commander Lowe, report to the bridge immediately," he ordered. "Commander Lowe to the bridge on the double."

Cowly moved close to Boxer. "Skipper, better lay it out for the Commander."

"I intend to," Boxer answered.

Cynthia came up to the bridge through the hatch. She wore the regulation coveralls and rain gear on top of it. "Commander Lowe, reporting as ordered," she said, saluting Boxer.

"Commander," Boxer said, "we don't salute aboard the *Turtle*, when it's under my command and I'm called skipper . . .you can dispense with the sir."

Cynthia nodded. "I'll try to remember that," she answered.

"One of the survivors," Boxer began, "is a pregnant woman."

"My God!" Cynthia exclaimed. "Is she alright?"

"She went into labor as soon as she was taken aboard. She's in the beginning of her eighth month and the MO isn't sure she's going to be able to have a normal birth. She might need a cesarian section and if she does, it will be done aboard."

"I'll do everything I can to help," Cynthia said.

Boxer nodded. He looked at Cowly; then back at Lowe. "The woman is black."

"You didn't have to tell me that," Cynthia said. "I wouldn't care what color—" she stopped.

"You guessed right. She is the woman I was going to marry. . . . She's married now."

Cynthia glared at him.

"Now she's just a woman in difficulty," Boxer said softly. "Another woman might make it easier for her."

"And who the hell will make it easier for me?" Cynthia asked through clenched teeth.

"No one," Boxer said.

151

"I'll go," Cynthia told him. "But not because you asked. I'll go because if I don't, I'll have trouble sleeping at night."

"Thanks," Boxer said.

"Is that all, *sir*?" Lowe asked.

"That's all, Commander." Boxer added. He knew she'd never call him skipper.

Cynthia saluted him.

He returned the salute. "She's in the OR," he said. "Tell the Doc that you have my permission to be with her."

Cynthia did an about face and hurried down the hatch.

"Skipper, is something going on that I should know about?" Bush asked.

"It's a personal matter," Boxer said.

"I never knew that Commanders could be so beautiful," Bush said.

"I'll introduce you to her later," Boxer said.

"That is some kind of a woman," Cowly commented.

Boxer gave him a questioning look.

Cowly flushed and turned away.

Boxer was about to apologize when the MO keyed him. "We've got to go for the cesarian, Skipper," he said.

"What do you need?"

"A couple of hands and a steady deck," the MO said.

"Will Commander Lowe help?"

"Yes. She volunteered as soon as I told her the situation, but I'll need two maybe three more."

"They'll be in OR in five minutes," Boxer said. He switched on the MC. "Now hear this . . . Now hear this . . . This is the Captain speaking . . . I need three volunteers to assist the doc in a cesarian section . . . Three volunteers report to the Sick Bay."

"I'll go," Cowly said.

"Negative," Boxer responded. "I need you on the bridge. We're going to dive."

152

"Dive?" Bush asked.

"The doc needs a stable deck and that's what he's going to get," Boxer said.

"But we're practically in the middle of the damn channel," Bush said.

"We're going to dive," Boxer said; then, turning to the junior officers on watch, he ordered the topside bridge cleared; then he keyed the COMMO. "Patch me through to Commander Williams," he said.

"Aye, aye, Skipper," the COMMO answered.

In a few moments Williams was on the radio.

"Commander, this is Captain Boxer . . . I'm going to dive—"

"Dive?"

"I got to give my MO a stable deck . . . Now listen to me . . . I have to go straight down. I'll stay down as long as I have to. It will be your job to keep all shipping away. I don't want any vessel closer than five thousand yards. Do not permit the *Silver Star* to get underway until we have surfaced."

"But—"

"Listen, Commander, I don't have time to play games. I have given you a direct order. Do you understand that?"

"Roger, I understand."

"I'll be in radio contact," Boxer said.

"Roger that," Williams answered.

Boxer switched on the MC. "All hands, stand by . . . Prepare to dive . . . Prepare to dive!" Then he secured the MC, switched control to the main bridge, and dropping through the hatch, he dogged it shut.

Within moments Boxer was on the bridge. He switched on the UWIS. "Smooth down below," he commented.

"My guess is that there's a good current down there," Bush said.

"Cowly, get me a depth reading," Boxer said.

"Aye, aye, sir," Cowly answered.

Boxer keyed the MO. "Have you got your volunteers?"

"Affirmative. Now give me a stable deck as quickly as you can," the MO said.

"Roger that," Boxer answered.

"Skipper," Cowly said, "four four feet."

Boxer keyed the DO. "We have a depth of four four feet. We'll go to the bottom. . . . Stand by."

"Cowly, give me a current reading as soon as we touch bottom," Boxer said.

"Aye, aye, Skipper," Cowly answered.

Boxer pushed the klaxon button three times. Then he keyed the DO. "Go to the bottom," he said.

"Roger that. . . . Flooding main ballast tanks."

The *Turtle* began to sink.

Boxer watched the instruments on the COMCOMP. "Might as well do some systems checking," he said, changing the position of several switches that gave him instant readings on the air filter system, the blower system and the ballast control valves.

"Down two zero feet," the DO reported.

Boxer checked the DDRO. It read twenty feet.

The Damage Control Officer keyed Boxer. "Looking good, Skipper,"

"Roger that," Boxer answered.

The DO keyed Boxer. "Passing through three zero feet."

This time Boxer checked the manual diving gauge above the COMCOMP. It registered thirty feet.

Boxer keyed the DO. "Put her down easy . . . Keep her trimmed."

"Roger that," the DO said.

Boxer turned to Cowly. "So far so good," he said.

Cowly smiled.

"Touching bottom," the DO reported. "Four four

154

feet . . . Trimming boat."

"Roger that," Boxer said.

"Skipper, current running at zero six knots," Cowly reported.

Boxer keyed the EO. "We have a zero six knot current . . . Give me enough power to hold the boat in one place."

"Aye, aye, Skipper," the EO said. "Applying power now."

Boxer keyed the MO. "Deck is stable," Boxer said.

"We've begun," the MO said.

"Skipper," the COMMO said, "Commander Williams is on the radio."

"Patch him through," Boxer answered. He already had drunk two cups of black coffee and was about to start pacing.

"Captain," Williams said, "another storm system is coming into the bay area. . . . Its ETA is sixteen hundred hours."

Boxer checked the COMCOMP's digital clock. It read 08:21:06. "With any luck we should be on our way again."

"Roger that. . . . How are things going?"

"No word yet from the MO," Boxer answered.

"Ten four," Williams answered.

Boxer switched off the radio interface control, stood up and stretched; then he sat down again. He had loved Louise and had been deeply hurt by her. That she had disappeared without a trace had always puzzled him.

"Skipper," Cowly said, "I'm going into the mess area. How about something to eat?"

"Not a bad idea," Bush commented. "Would you bring me another cup of coffee and ham an' eggs."

"Sure. Skipper?"

"Ham an' eggs will do fine," Boxer answered.

"I'm on my way," Cowly said.

Bush moved closer to Boxer. "Cowly's one damn fine officer."

"The best," Boxer answered.

"I don't mean to pry," Bush said, "but when a woman is concerned, I always think it's best to know as much about the situation as possible."

Boxer gave him a quizzical look. "What woman and what situation?"

"Commander Lowe," Bush responded.

"What about the commander?" Boxer asked.

"Is there something, or was there something going on between her and Cowly?" Bush asked.

Boxer wasn't sure whether he should laugh or not. He decided to keep a straight face.

"I saw the look you gave Cowly when he commented that she was some kind of woman," Bush said.

"Oh?"

"I don't want to become the third party," Bush said. "I want to meet her and—"

"And make a play for her?"

Bush nodded. "Despite your opinion of me, I can be charming."

"My opinion of you has nothing to do with your charm, or your courage, or your professionalism."

"We're just different style sailors," Bush said. "I run a very tight ship, you run—" He smiled. "I was going to say a loose one, but that's not true."

"Well, at least you've learned that much," Boxer responded.

"What about Lowe and Cowly?"

"Nothing about them," Boxer said. "Absolutely nothing about them."

Bush rubbed his hands. "Excellent. Excellent. She is really as Cowly said, 'Some kind of woman!'"

Boxer didn't answer.

The MO keyed Boxer. "Mother and daughter doing fine," he said.

Boxer cleared his throat. "Roger that," he said and immediately relayed the good news to the men on the bridge. Then he switched on the MC. "Now hear this . . . All hands now hear this . . . This is the captain speaking . . . A few moments ago a girl was born aboard our boat."

A cheer sounded through the length of the *Turtle*.

"I don't remember a child ever being born on an American submarine, or any other submarine, so I guess this is some kind of a first."

Another cheer went up.

"Mother and child are doing fine," Boxer continued. "I'll report further on the situation . . . Ten four."

"Too bad we can't have a real celebration," Cowly said.

"Who says we can't?" Boxer responded and he keyed the Chief in charge of the kitchen, which was designed and operated exactly the same as the *Shark*'s. "Chief, I want you to do some fancy baking and serve up the ice cream we have aboard."

"Aye, aye, Skipper," the Chief answered.

Boxer keyed the MO. "Is it safe to surface now? . . . Another storm is due to hit the bay area at fourteen hundred hours."

"You can go up and down like a yo-yo," the MO said.

"I'll be there as soon as I can," Boxer told him; then he keyed the COMMO, "Contact Commander Williams."

"Aye, aye, sir," the COMMO said.

A moment later Williams was on the radio.

"Mother and daughter are doing fine," Boxer said.

"You sound like the proud father," Williams laughed.

157

"By the way the father, Doctor Henry Fowler, has been in radio phone contact with me. He's howling mad that you have his wife aboard your boat."

"If I were him, I would be too. Next time he calls, tell him he has a healthy daughter."

"Will do."

"Okay, we're surfacing in one five minutes. We will break water off your stern. I don't want any shipping closer than five thousand yards. Have your men stand by to take off the survivors."

"Roger that," Williams answered. "By the way, I have a box of very good cigars."

"That's fine," Boxer said. "Over." Then he turned and saw Cynthia.

"She's asking for you," Cynthia said.

"Thanks again for helping—"

She waved him silent. "Captain, may I return to what I was doing," Cynthia asked.

"Yes," Boxer said with a nod.

She saluted him.

Feeling ridiculous, Boxer returned the salute; then he said to Bush, "Take the CONN. . . . I'll be back in ten minutes."

"Aye, aye, Skipper," Bush said.

Boxer left the bridge and hurried into the Sick Bay area.

When Boxer approached her, Louise opened her eyes.

She smiled up at him and reaching for his hand, she said, "You're a wonderful man, Jack."

Boxer was at a loss. He didn't know what to say or do. Part of him wanted to sweep her into his arms, while the other part recognized that now she was another man's wife and the mother of that man's child.

"I know what you're feeling," she said softly, "because I feel the same thing."

"Better sleep now. In a matter of minutes we'll be on

158

the surface and you'll be transferred to a Coast Guard Cutter and then to a hospital ashore. Your husband is frantic and has been on the radio phone with the captain of one of the cutters."

"He's a good man, Jack," Louise said.

"He'd have to be if you married him," Boxer answered.

"It's best this way," Louise said.

Boxer wasn't going to admit to that. He didn't honestly know whether it was "best."

"Would you mind if I asked you a special favor?" Louise questioned.

"Ask and then I'll tell you if I mind or not."

"Would you stand as my child's godfather?"

Boxer smiled. "I'd be honored," he said. "Truly honored."

She squeezed his hand.

"I think it's the first time a child was born in a submerged submarine," Boxer said.

She closed her eyes.

"Better rest—"

Suddenly the *Turtle* rolled to the port side.

Instantly Boxer keyed the bridge. "Bush, what was that?"

"We've got a red signal on the port drive shaft system," Bush said.

"Stand by," Boxer said. He keyed the DCO. "What have you got on the port drive shaft system?"

"An overheat, Skipper."

"Roger that," Boxer answered and he keyed the EO. "Have you any malfunction signal on the port drive shaft system?"

"Came on a few secs ago," the EO answered.

"Roger that," Boxer answered.

The DCO keyed Boxer. "Skipper, something is slowing the shaft . . . The problem is external . . . All parts of the internal system are green."

"Roger that," Boxer answered. He keyed the EO. "Disengage the port drive shaft."

"Aye, aye, Skipper," the EO answered.

"I have to go now," Boxer said, looking down at Louise.

Her eyes were wide with fear. "Everything is going to be alright, isn't it?"

"Just a slight problem. Nothing to worry about," Boxer said.

"That the truth, Jack?"

"The truth," he lied. "I'll be back as soon as it's straightened out, but meanwhile you get some rest."

She nodded, kissed the back of his hand and looking up at him, she said. "I still love you, Jack. I still love you."

"And I love you," he answered, gently kissing her forehead.

Twelve

Just as Boxer reached the bridge, the *Turtle* was violently wrenched to the starboard.

The COMCOMP's red signal indicator for the starboard drive shaft system began to flash.

"I have the CONN," Boxer said.

Bush left the captain's chair and stepped away from the COMCOMP.

Boxer switched on the SYSDCONET. The starboard drive shaft was overheating. He keyed the EO. "Disengage the starboard drive shaft."

"Aye, aye, Skipper," the EO responded.

Boxer switched on the UWIS and the underwater high intensity lights.

"Skipper," Cowly said, "we're beginning to drift to the port side."

"Roger that," Boxer answered. "Monitor the port side UWIS," he said.

"Aye, aye, Skipper," Cowly said.

"I don't see anything," Boxer commented, moving aside to let Bush view the screen.

"Nothing," Bush said.

"We can scan three hundred and sixty degrees under us, but not along our own hull," Boxer growled. He switched on the MD. "Commander Lowe report to the

161

bridge on the double," he barked out. Then to Bush, he said, "Maybe the commander can tell us what the fuck is going on."

Within seconds, Cynthia reported to Boxer.

He pointed to the SYSDCONET. "The drive shaft systems are out—both overheated."

"Not likely," Cynthia answered, "unless something was braking them."

"Meaning that something has fouled both?" Boxer asked.

"Yes, sir."

Boxer pointed to the UWIS screen. "I can see in every direction," he said, "except along the boat's hull."

"I'll recommend that modification, sir," she said calmly.

"Your recommendation won't help us now," Boxer replied.

"Skipper," Cowly said. "We're going to be expected topside in five minutes."

Boxer nodded and keyed the COMMO. "Get Captain Williams," he said.

"Aye, aye, Skipper," the COMMO answered.

"Williams here," the Commander said.

"Captain, we've got a problem down here," Boxer told him.

"Roger that," Williams said. "Standing by."

"Ten four," Boxer responded. Again he switched on the MC. "Vargas to the bridge on the double."

"Skipper," Cowly said, "there's a drop off on the port side."

Boxer changed the position of two switches and the portside came up on the screen. He keyed the SO. "Can you give me a distance reading on the portside."

"Clean sweep for max range," the SO answered.

"Use a cosecant square pattern," Boxer told him.

"Same, Skipper," the SO answered.

"Roger that," Boxer said.

Vargas reported. "I need two men to go out and find out what is grabbing our drive shafts."

"I'll go and take one of the new men with me," Vargas said.

Boxer nodded.

"Give me ten minutes," Vargas said.

"You've got it," Boxer told him.

"Skipper," Cowly said, "we're getting very close to the drop-off point."

"We'll just have to sit tight," Boxer answered. "If we start to go over the edge, I'll surface without any power—but I don't like doing that."

After a few minutes, Vargas keyed Boxer. "Skipper, we're going out through the port pressure chamber. We're using conventional scuba, except for the radio."

"Roger that," Boxer answered. He knew Vargas chose the conventional gear because it would be familiar to the new man. The COMCOMP indicated when the pressure chamber was flooded and when it was opened to the sea, a green light began to flash. "They're out," Boxer announced and turned his attention to the UWIS.

Vargas keyed Boxer. "We've grabbed a metal fishing net."

"A fishing net?" Boxer questioned.

"And several hundred feet of zero five inch metal cable."

"On both shafts?"

"Affirmative. Skipper, we'll need two teams to cut it away."

"Roger that," Boxer said. "Stand by to direct teams."

"Aye, aye, Skipper," Vargas answered.

Boxer turned to Bush. "I need two underwater burn teams to rid us of the stuff we've picked up on our shafts."

"Aye, aye, Skipper, I'll have those teams out there as

soon as possible."

"Better make it sooner than that," Cowly said. "We're continuing to move."

Boxer keyed Williams and told him what the problem was. "We should be able to move within three zero minutes."

"Contact me before you begin," Williams said. "The sky is getting dark again."

"Still the same info on the storm?"

"Nothing has changed," Williams answered.

"Ten four," Boxer said.

"Burn teams out," Bush reported.

Boxer turned to Cynthia. "Will the SYSDCONET show if the drive shafts have been bent?"

"Each shaft is electronically monitored," she answered.

Vargas keyed Boxer. "Burning has begun, Skipper."

"Roger that."

Boxer keyed the EO. "Stand by to apply power."

"Aye, aye, Skipper," the EO answered.

Vargas keyed Boxer. "Starboard shaft free."

"Roger that," Boxer said and reported the condition to the officers on the bridge.

"Skipper, a few revs and a left full rudder will take us away from the drop-off point," Cowly said.

Boxer keyed Vargas. "How much longer on the port shaft?"

"A few minutes . . . zero five at the very most," Vargas answered.

"Roger that," Boxer said. "Vargas says zero five minutes at the outside."

Cowly nodded. "We're still moving."

Boxer didn't answer. He was gambling that it would take the *Turtle* longer than five minutes to reach the drop-off point.

"I sure could use a cup of coffee," Bush commented.

"So could I," Cowly said.

"Skipper, would you like coffee?" Bush asked.

"Sure would," Boxer answered.

"Commander," Bush said, "would you—"

Vargas keyed Boxer. "Port side shaft freed."

"Roger that," Boxer said. "Get your men back inside."

Suddenly the *Turtle* rolled to the starboard.

"Christ we're dropping!" Cowly exclaimed.

Boxer keyed the EO. "Full power."

The *Turtle* shuddered and began to move forward.

Vargas keyed Boxer. "What the fuck is happening, Skipper?"

"Stand by," Boxer said. "We'll settle down again."

"Roger that," Vargas said.

Boxer keyed the DO. "I got six zero feet on my depth gauge."

"Same, Skipper," the DO answered.

"Make four zero feet and hold it steady."

Making four zero feet and holding steady," the DO said.

Boxer keyed Vargas. "Come aboard as soon as we touch bottom," Boxer said.

"Roger that," Vargas said.

"Helmsman," Boxer said, "come to course two six degrees."

"Coming to course two six degrees," Mahony answered.

Boxer keyed the EO. "Stand by to stop all engines."

"Standing by to stop all engines."

Boxer keyed Williams. "Stand by. We'll be surfacing in approximately one zero minutes."

"Roger that. The cigars are waiting for you."

"Ten four," Boxer answered; then he turned to Bush, and said, "As soon as Vargas and the burn teams are aboard, take the CONN and bring her up—"

Bush took his position at the COMCOMP and switched

on the MC. "Now hear this . . . Now hear this . . . Stand by to retrieve personnel . . . Stand by to retrieve personnel."

Boxer nodded and left the bridge.

"Mrs. Fowler resisted the sedation," the MO said. "She's been asking for you."

Boxer nodded and hurried to Louise's bed. "Are you alright?" he asked, bending close to her.

"Are you?"

"I'm fine," he answered. "We'll be surfacing in a few minutes; then you'll be on your way to a hospital."

"Jack, can you stay with me until—"

"Until we break water," he said. "Then I'll be needed on the bridge."

She nodded.

"Are you comfortable?" he asked.

"As comfortable as a person can be who has stitches from her belly button to her—"

The COMMO keyed Boxer. "Commander Williams is on the radio."

"Patch him through," Boxer said.

"Captain the CNO and someone named Kinkade are coming aboard. They want to speak to you as soon as you surface."

"Roger that," Boxer said.

Louise took hold of Boxer's hand. "You're a very different man here," she said. "I know you're brave, but here you're full of authority. You're in command—there's no doubt about that."

Boxer smiled. "I sure as hell hope not."

"All personnel aboard," Bush announced over the MC. "Stand by to surface."

"How long will that take?" Louise asked.

"A few minutes," Boxer answered.

166

The klaxon sounded twice.

"That's the signal that we're surfacing," Boxer said.

Louise nodded. "I have something to tell you," she said. "But you must promise me not to become angry. I know what you can do when you become angry."

Boxer nodded.

"No, say it."

"I promise I won't become angry."

"I left you because I was asked to. Two men came to me and told me that it would be better for everyone if I never saw you again."

"Kinkade!" Boxer exclaimed, starting to stand.

"No, you promised me that you wouldn't do or say anything," she said, gripping his hand tightly.

Boxer sat down again.

"It really was for the best," Louise said. "Your world is still a very white one."

He didn't say anything.

"Are you very angry with me?"

"No," Boxer said gently.

"Please don't be angry with anyone else," Louise told him. "It worked out for the best. I'm married to a good man."

"Do you love him?"

She smiled. "Yes, I love him. Do you have someone you love?"

"Yes," Boxer said with a nod.

"I'm happy for you," Louise said.

Bush's voice came over the MC. "Ten seconds to surfacing."

"I've got to go," Boxer said. He kissed Louise on the lips. "I'll see you before you're transferred," he said.

"Six seconds," Bush said, "and counting."

Boxer smiled at Louise, turned, and headed for the secondary bridge.

"Surface . . . Surface . . . Surface," Bush said over

the MC.

Boxer was the first to crack the hatch and push it open. He clambered up the remaining ladder steps, lifted himself up through the hatch, and took his position at the AUXCOMCOMP.

The wind was brisk. There was a good chop in the bay and the sky was lead gray.

Boxer keyed Bush. "I have the CONN. You and mister Cowly come topside."

"Roger that," Bush answered.

The *Turtle* had surfaced a thousand yards astern of the cutters, and Boxer ordered a course change that would bring her alongside of one of them. Then he switched on the MC. "Deck detail topside. Stand by to transfer civilian personnel to cutters."

The COMMO keyed Boxer. "The CNO and Mr. Kinkade request permission to come aboard."

"Permission denied until all civilian personnel are transferred," Boxer said.

"Aye, aye, Skipper," the COMMO said.

Boxer keyed the EO. "Stop all engines."

"Stopping all engines," the EO said.

"Mahony," Boxer called out, "she's in your hands. Bring her in as close as you can."

"Aye, aye, Skipper," the helmsman said.

Boxer keyed the COMMO. "Get me Commander Williams."

"Aye, aye, Skipper."

A few moments later Williams was on the radio.

"Commander, have your men stand by to secure the lines from the *Turtle* and to take aboard the civilians."

"Roger that," Williams said. "You can tell Mrs. Fowler that her husband is aboard and anxious to see her."

"Is that the same Fowler who played ball for Columbia?"

"Best college quarterback to come out of Columbia in thirty years," Williams said.

"I thought the name sounded familiar," Boxer commented.

"He says he wants to meet you."

"Give him a number. There's a couple that come before him."

"I'm sure he'll wait his turn."

"Ten four," Boxer answered with a laugh. "Ten four."

Boxer remained on the *Turtle*'s bridge until all of the survivors, with the exception of Louise, were safely transferred to the cutters. When her turn came, he turned the CONN over to Bush and went down to the deck.

"Your husband is aboard the cutter," he told her.

She nodded.

"He wants to meet me," Boxer said.

"I think you'll like him, Jack."

Boxer smiled and took hold of her hand. "I'll go aboard with you."

The MO came on deck with the baby.

"I'll carry her," Boxer said, taking the child into his arms.

"Thank you doctor," Louise said, looking up at the MO.

He bent down and kissed her forehead. "Good luck Mrs. Fowler," he said.

Boxer turned to the two crewmen who were standing by. "Take Mrs. Fowler aboard the cutter."

"Aye, aye, Skipper," the two of them answered.

Boxer leaped from one moving deck to the other. Dr. Fowler was waiting on the cutter with Captain Williams, Stark and Kinkade.

"Your daughter," Boxer said, handing the baby to

its father.

Louise was brought aboard.

"Are you alright?" Fowler asked.

She nodded. "I'm fine. Just a bit tired."

Fowler nodded. "You're going to be flown to the Norfolk General Hospital."

Louise nodded.

"Well, Captain," Fowler said, "I heard a great deal about you."

"Captain," Stark said, "I apologize for interrupting but—"

"You'll excuse me, Doctor," Boxer said. "I don't have the time now to chat. Perhaps if you'll wait—"

"I'll be going with Louise," Fowler said.

"I promised your wife that I'd stand as godfather to the child."

"Did she ask you to?"

"Yes. But if you have any objections, I naturally would respect them."

"We live in Cincinnati, but in two or three weeks we'll be moving to Washington."

"I'll find you," Boxer said, looking directly at Kinkade.

Fowler extended his hand. "I'm angry as hell at you," he said. "But Louise is alive and I have a beautiful child." He smiled. "It's too hard for me to be angry now. Maybe later."

Boxer shook his hand. "I hope not," he replied; then turning to Stark and Kinkade he said, "You have permission to board the *Turtle*."

Kinkade glared at him.

Boxer, Stark and Kinkade were crowded into Boxer's quarters, which, though larger than those he had aboard the *Shark*, were still small.

Stark sat at the desk. Kinkade took the other chair and Boxer sat on his bunk.

"You've lost precious time," Kinkade said.

"I've saved precious lives," Boxer counted, "including the life of a woman who is still very dear to me."

"Exactly what happened?" Stark asked.

"We had the aircraft on the scope; then suddenly the RO reported that it was falling. The May Day came within seconds, and we were the closest vessel. Mrs. Fowler needed a cesarian section and the MO needed a stable deck."

"So you submerged," Kinkade said.

Boxer nodded. "That was the only way to give him a stable deck. We went down to four zero feet to hold the *Turtle* steady and, to keep from drifting, we were under some power."

"Enough to pick up a metal fishing net and its cables," Kinkade said sourly.

"So far," Stark said, "he can't be faulted for anything he did."

"He's almost a full twenty-four hours behind schedule," Kinkade said. "I wanted him well out to sea by now. I don't like the way this operation has begun."

"Look, Kinkade," Boxer said suddenly flaring. "I could be underway now, but you're here jabbering about nonsense. That plane went down and I wasn't going to leave its survivors in the water. You should know me by now."

"I know you," Kinkade said. "You do exactly what you want to do, regardless of the rules."

"I do what I must do. Now, if you don't like it, you can have me replaced. Bush is aboard; let him take the *Turtle* on this mission."

"I have given that possibility a great deal of thought."

Boxer looked at Stark. "That man is out of his fucking head."

Kinkade stood up. "I want him relieved, as of now."

"That's fine with me," Boxer said. "I haven't even unpacked my gear."

"Admiral," Kinkade said, "will you give the necessary order." He was red in the face.

"No," Stark said quietly. "I once told you that you operate your people and I will operate mine." He stood up. "Captain, proceed as previously ordered."

"Aye, aye, sir," Boxer answered.

Kinkade left the chair and stormed out of the cabin.

"He's getting worse," Boxer said.

Stark nodded. "I think he's more upset with your relationship to his granddaughter than he lets on . . . He thinks you're completely immoral."

Boxer laughed. "He thinks I'm sleeping with Trish to get back at him?"

"Something like that, I guess."

Boxer shook his head. "He's going to have to come to terms with it on his own. There's nothing I or Trish can do to help him. And, frankly, I don't feel like helping him do anything. I saved his life. That's enough. It's probably more than he'd do for me."

"Then Louise told you?" Stark asked.

Boxer nodded. "I promised I wouldn't do anything about it—and I won't."

Stark stood up.

"Did you know about—"

"Only after he had done it," Stark said.

"It's really very hard to like that man," Boxer commented.

"I don't try anymore," Stark said, walking to the door and opening it.

Boxer followed him and together they went topside. Kinkade was already on the cutter's deck.

"Good luck," Stark said. "You're going to need it."

"That's reassuring," Boxer answered.

"Just the truth," Stark said, leaping across the narrow ribbon of water separating the two bobbing hulls.

Boxer saluted him and he returned the courtesy.

"Captain," Captain Williams called from the deck. "Here are those cigars I promised you." And he tossed the box toward the deck.

Boxer made an easy one-handed catch.

"Good going," Williams said.

Boxer waved and keying Bush, he said, "Stand by to get underway."

"Aye, aye, Skipper," Bush answered.

Boxer looked back at the cutter and waved.

As soon as the *Turtle* passed beneath the Chesapeake Bay Bridge, Boxer switched on the MC. "Now hear this . . . All hands, now hear this . . . This is the Captain speaking . . . Congratulations on the way you handled the crisis situation . . . Half the crew is new to my command and we are all new to this boat . . . There are things about her that we'll have to learn together. She is, as you must realize, like no other submarine in the world. She has been designed for a particular type of mission, and this leads me to why all of us are aboard the *Turtle.* . . .

"This is not just a shake down cruise . . . We are sailing under sealed orders which will be opened at the specified time. We are on a mission, and because we are on a mission, your attention to every detail of your job could mean the difference between life and death—your own and those of your shipmates . . . To the new members of the crew, and the old, welcome aboard."

"I didn't know you liked to speechify," Cowly grinned.

Boxer rolled his eyes; then he hit the klaxon three times and switched on the MC again. "Prepare to dive . . . Prepare to dive . . . Prepare to dive . . . Clear

173

the bridge . . . All hands, clear the bridge."

Bush, Cowly, two junior officers and Mahony scrambled down the hatchway. Boxer followed and dogged the hatch closed. Within moments he was at the COMCOMP. He keyed the DO. "Make five zero feet."

"Aye, aye, Skipper . . . Making five zero feet," the DO answered.

As soon as the forward and main ballast flood valves were opened, the hissing sound of escaping air filled the *Turtle*.

Boxer watched the COMCOMP instruments. The DO wasn't using the dive planes.

"Passing through one zero feet," the DO reported.

Boxer keyed the SO. "Report all targets that come within a security range of three thousand yards."

"Marking a security range of three thousand yards," the SO answered.

Boxer keyed the EO. "Make one five knots."

"Making one five knots," the EO answered.

"Passing through twenty feet," the DO said.

"Roger that," Boxer answered.

The Damage Control Officer keyed Boxer. "Skipper, all systems green."

"Roger that," Boxer answered. He switched on the UWIS. They were above a meandering valley.

"Three zero feet," the DO said.

"Roger that," Boxer responded and checked the DDRO; then the depth gauge above the COMCOMP. Both registered thirty feet.

"Trimming," the DO said.

Boxer watched the Electronic Bubble Indicator move to a null.

"Dive completed," the DO said.

"Roger that," Boxer answered. Then he turned to Cowly and Bush. "We'll divide the CONN between us. Cowly, you make up the schedule so that we don't pull the same hours. Cowly, put Commander Lowe on stand by in case any of us should need her assistance."

"Aye, aye, Skipper," Cowly answered.

"Pick three officers to act as our EXO," Boxer said. "Better take two from the *Shark*'s crew and one from the new men."

"Which of us has the CONN now?" Bush asked.

"Toss a coin," Boxer said. "I'm going to get something to eat, and then I'm going to sleep for a while."

"Skipper, you forgot about the ice cream and cake," Cowly laughed.

"Damned if I didn't!" Boxer exclaimed and he keyed the mess Chief. "How is the ice cream and cake coming?" he asked.

"Should be ready in zero five minutes, Skipper," the Chief told him.

"I'll be down to sample it," Boxer said.

"Anytime, Skipper," the Chief answered.

Boxer switched on the MC. "Cake, coffee and ice cream will be available to all crew members in five minutes," he said, as Cowly and Bush played toss for the CONN. "Section chiefs rotate your men . . . Allow them to eat and drink on station . . . This is a special occasion . . . We're celebrating the birth of a child aboard the *Turtle*."

"I have the CONN," Cowly said.

Boxer nodded, stood up and left the COMCOMP. "See you in a few hours."

"Mind if I join you?" Bush asked.

"Come along," Boxer said.

"Have you any idea what our orders might be?" Bush questioned.

"None," Boxer said.

The two men walked into the mess area.

"What about Lowe?" Bush asked.

"What about her?"

175

"You know what I mean," Bush said.

"She's engaged to be married," Boxer answered.

"That doesn't count. Even if she were married it wouldn't count."

Boxer was surprised by Bush's attitude. When it came to his involvement with women, he had always figured him to be "by the rules" just as the man was with everything else.

The Chief, a broad shouldered man with a red face, came out of the kitchen. "I baked three kinds of cake; apple pie, plain pound cake, and something called bobka."

"The men will be coming for it soon," Boxer said.

"I have it all set up. My helpers will bring it out and the men will take it themselves."

"Good," Boxer said. "But before I sample your cake, I want to have something to eat."

"I'm starved too," Cowly said.

Each of them used their food key card and selected what he wanted.

Boxer chose a fish and vegetable dish, while Bush picked a chicken dish.

The members of the crew began to drift into the mess area and the Chief set out the huge trays of cake and containers of ice cream.

"Lowe is some kind of an authority on this boat, isn't she?" Bush asked.

"She is *the* authority on it," Boxer answered.

Bush nodded.

The two of them finished eating without additional conversation. Both had cake and ice cream. Boxer tried the bobka and liked it. Bush had the apple pie.

When Boxer left the mess area he went straight to his quarters, where he undressed, showered and then stretched out in his bunk for a few hours sleep.

He awoke with a start.

Bush was keying him. "Skipper, we're coming up to one hundred miles."

"Roger that," Boxer said. "Pass the CONN to your acting EXO and you and Cowly report to my quarters."

"Aye, aye, Skipper," Bush answered.

Boxer washed his face, cleaned his teeth and was dressed by the time Bush and Cowly arrived. "I wanted you to witness the fact that I'm opening the ship's safe and removing our sealed orders."

Neither man said anything.

Boxer took the envelope out of the safe, slit it open and withdrew the orders. "I'll skip the boilerplate and get straight to our assignment," he said and he began to read. "The *Turtle* will rendezvous with the freighter, the *African Star*, at North Lat. 37°, 20° West Long. at approximately 0300 on the 13th day of Sept. and take aboard Mr. Julio Sanchez, who will act as guide to the men of your strike force. The *Turtle* will put ashore a strike force at North Lat. 35°, 20° East Long. This force will then proceed inland under Mr. Sanchez's direction to the prison camp of El Ka Rish, where the strike force will liberate the prisoners held in said camp and bring them to the *Turtle*. The *Turtle* will then return to its home base."

Cowly gave a long, low whistle.

"Where the hell is it?" Bush asked.

"Somewhere on the Libyan coast in the Gulf of Sidra I'd guess from the coordinates," Boxer answered.

"They must be nuts!" Bush exclaimed.

Boxer nodded. "They probably are."

"How the hell did Sanchez become involved?" Cowly asked.

Boxer shook his head. "The ways of Sanchez are indeed mysterious," he said.

177

"The Spic isn't going to like this one," Cowly commented.

"Neither do I," Boxer said. "Believe me, neither do I."

"So much for hoping this would be an easy one," Bush said.

"Alright," Boxer said, "I'll brief the Spic. But consider the orders top secret. Nothing to the crew or any of the other officers until I make a general announcement, which will be after we pick up Sanchez and I know something more about the land operation."

Cowly and Bush nodded.

"Bush, I want you to start to get satellite photos of the Libyan coast; then details of our landing point. I want to know everything about the area, and I mean *everything*— from the type of seabed to the kind of crops grown by the natives."

"Aye, aye, Skipper," Bush answered.

"Cowly," Boxer said, "I want a complete military assessment of what kind of opposition we can expect. That's everything on, or under the sea, on land and in the air."

"Aye, aye, Skipper," Cowly answered.

Thirteen

Boxer put the *Turtle* through her paces and in every way she proved to be an exceptional boat. But he deferred the two most severe tests until after he had rendezvoused with the *African Star* and Sanchez was aboard.

Immediately after Boxer had opened and read the sealed orders, the crew was put on alert status and a rigorous regimen of training began.

The following day, Boxer called Vargas to his quarters and offered him one of the cigars Commander Williams had given to him.

Vargas used his thumb nail to cut the end of the cigar, lit up and said, "Next you'll ask me to sit down."

Boxer nodded and pointed to the chair.

Vargas sat down. "Now I need a good stiff drink."

"I have vodka, if you want one," Boxer said.

"I thought the regs said no booze."

"They do," Boxer answered. "But the Captain has the right—"

"Okay, Skipper, stop the soft soaping bit and tell me what the fuck is up."

Boxer opened his drawer, took out a detailed map of the Libyan coast and, pointing to a spot already marked with a red circle, he said, "That's where we're going, and that's where you and your men are going to make a landing."

"No shit!" Vargas exclaimed, blowing a cloud of smoke

off to one side.

"Some miles from the coast is a prison camp. You and your men will free the prisoners and bring them back to the *Turtle*."

Vargas blew another cloud of smoke but this time it was directed toward the ceiling. "What fucking idiot comes up with these ideas?" he asked.

"Spic, I know it's not Stark. It could be Kinkade, or it could be someone in the State Department. But it doesn't matter who it is, does it?"

"Nah," Vargas answered. "But letting us know little things like: how far is the camp from the coast, and how many men are defending it—things like that would be real helpful if they want us to stay alive."

"We'll know more when we pick up Sanchez," Boxer said.

Vargas's eyes opened wide. "How the fuck is he involved?"

Boxer shrugged. "I don't know, but he is, and he's going to be your guide to the camp."

"Hey Skipper, who pays that guy?" Vargas asked.

"I sure as hell don't know," Boxer answered. "Someone must. Julio lives pretty damn well, even for a millionaire."

"When do I tell my men?" Vargas asked.

"I'll tell the entire crew after Sanchez is aboard," Boxer said. "After that you can handle it any way you want."

"What about a practice landing?"

"No time. You do it and it's the real thing," Boxer said.

"Skipper, I'll have that drink if you don't mind," Vargas said.

"Sure," Boxer said, "and I'll join you."

Boxer had the CONN. He sat at the COMCOMP and

scanned the instruments. Everything was normal. In his mind's eye he pictured the maps that Bush and Cowly had collected for him. The landing would be taking place along a very rocky piece of coast. The bottom was steep, and a thousand yards from the shore it dropped to seven hundred feet. An eight to ten knot current moved from west to east. That was going to make it difficult to keep the *Turtle* steady when the assault team went ashore. He figured they would leave the *Turtle* in thirty feet of water and make their way up the beach from that depth. No matter how he looked at it, just putting the men ashore was going to be a problem and— He heard a noise behind him and turned.

"Captain, I request permission to speak to you," Cynthia said.

"Permission granted," Boxer replied.

"I would prefer to do it in your quarters, sir," she said.

"Lipner," Boxer said, speaking to Lieutenant Commander Paul Lipner, the acting EXO on this shift, "take the CONN. Keep her steady as she goes. I'll be in my quarters for a few minutes."

"Aye, aye, Skipper," Lipner said.

Boxer nodded. Lipner was one of the new men aboard, and from what Boxer could see, he was a first rate officer. Cowly had made an excellent choice. Boxer turned to Cynthia. "My quarters Commander," he said, gesturing to her to go before him.

A short while later Boxer closed the door behind him and pointed to the chair, while he sat down at the desk and switched on the MINICOMCOMP. "Before you begin," he said, "I have something I want to say to you. Aboard this boat, or any other boat I command, no officer is called sir. The men call me Skipper. I don't like being called sir."

"I will try to remember that," Cynthia answered, looking straight at him.

Boxer reached for a pipe, filled it, and as he lit it he said, "Now you tell me why you wanted to speak to me."

"I must ask that the conversation be kept absolutely confidential," Cynthia said.

Boxer nodded. "Any conversation between myself and a member of the crew has that status."

"Secondly," Cynthia said, "the particular status difference between us must not have anything to do with the conversation."

"Agreed," Boxer said, blowing smoke from the bowl of his pipe. He noticed that for the first time since she had come aboard she was not wearing her engagement ring.

Cynthia took a deep breath and slowly exhaled. "I'd like to know what you told Captain Bush about me?" she asked.

Boxer took the pipe out from between his lips. He had introduced her to Bush less than forty eight hours ago. "Did he say I said something about you?" he asked.

"No."

"Then why the question?"

"Because I know men talk about the women they fuck," she said, her eyes riveted to his.

"You should know me better than that," he said softly.

"May I smoke?" she asked.

"I am," he told her.

She removed a pack of cigarettes from her breast pocket. "He asked me," she said, "if he could visit me in my quarters. Only he didn't put it that way." She took a cigarette out of the pack and put it between her lips.

Boxer struck a match and held it out to her. "Just what did he say?" he asked.

"He said he wanted to fuck me," Cynthia said. "I told him that he was way off base and he answered, 'I know you fuck so don't play coy with me.'"

"Then what did you do?"

"I got up and left the table," Cynthia said.

"This took place in the mess area?"

She nodded and said, "Commander Cowly was at the next table. He must have guessed that something was wrong, because he came after me and asked if I was alright."

Boxer put the pipe back in his mouth and puffed hard on it.

"I like that man," Cynthia said.

"Cowly?"

"Yes. He's certainly several cuts above Bush."

"It's not like Bush—"

"Are you trying to tell me that you don't believe—"

"Nothing like that," Boxer assured her. "I don't doubt that it happened just the way you described it. In fact, I'd have been surprised if he didn't make some kind of an overture to you."

"I don't understand that," she said, flicking ashes off the end of the cigarette into an ash tray on the desk.

"I'm not sure I can explain it," Boxer told her. "But something is going on with Bush that's strange."

"He has his problems; I have mine, and I'm sure you have yours. I don't want to be the focus of his sexual needs."

"If it happens again," Boxer said, "I want you to report it immediately and bring him up on charges."

"That's pretty drastic, isn't it?"

"You or any other woman aboard should not be subjected to sexual insults," Boxer said.

"Can't it be handled differently?"

"If I speak to him, he'll know you spoke to me about it. That might provoke him even more. Something has gone wrong in his head about women. I don't think it's you alone. I think it's all women."

Cynthia put another cigarette into her mouth. "For your sake I hope that whatever has gone wrong doesn't spill over into other areas."

"So do I," Boxer said. "So do I."

Boxer returned to the bridge. "I have the CONN."

"Aye, aye, Skipper," Lipner answered.

Boxer scanned the instruments on the COMCOMP. All systems were green.

Cowly came up to the bridge.

"You're not due here for another two hours," Boxer said, looking at the digital clock.

"Couldn't sleep," Cowly answered.

"I know the feeling all too well," Boxer answered.

"What time are we scheduled to rendezvous?" he asked in a whisper.

"Just before you take the CONN," Boxer answered.

Cowly made no comment.

Boxer decided to take the proverbial bull by the horns. "Have you noticed anything different about Bush?" he asked.

Cowly hesitated; then he said, "He's looser than he was the last time he was aboard."

Boxer nodded. "That's certainly for the better. Anything else?"

"He's intent on getting into Commander Lowe's pants," Cowly said.

"Say again."

"He's coming down really heavy on her," Cowly answered.

"You've seen this?"

"I saw something," Cowly answered, "in the mess area. Whatever it was, it upset her. I went out after her to find out if she was okay. She said she was, but I could see that she was really shaken."

"Did you say anything to him about it?"

Cowly shook his head. "He said something to me later. He said that 'Lowe is a cunt, even if she wears

184

a uniform.' "

Boxer frowned.

"Personally, I think she is one hell of a woman," Cowly said, looking straight at Boxer. Then dropping his voice to a whisper again, he added, "Skipper, I *can* have feelings about a woman. I really can make love to one, too."

Boxer wasn't going to become involved in that kind of a discussion. He could trust Cowly, regardless of his sexual preferences. But he wasn't at all sure that he could trust Bush.

"To be honest, Skipper," Cowly said, "I don't know whether I like him loose any more than I did when he was tight."

"Would you keep an eye on him?" Boxer asked.

"I'm not sure I understand?"

"Let me know if you think his new found 'looseness' might be spilling over into other areas?"

Cowly became thoughtful and was silent for several moments before he said, "Given my own behavior, the shoe could very well be on the other foot."

"Not aboard any boat I command," Boxer answered.

"Thank you, Skipper," Cowly answered.

"Will you do what I asked?"

Cowly nodded.

"Keep an anecdotal record," Boxer said, looking away.

"Are you sure that's what you want me to do?"

"Positive," Boxer answered.

Cowly uttered a deep sigh. "Then you don't—or rather you *do* expect this to become more of a problem?"

"I sure as hell hope not," Boxer answered. "But I have to be prepared if it does. Remember, he has rank, and my attitude toward him is well known by the CNO and Kinkade."

"I wonder what the hell is going on in his head?" Cowly asked. "I mean why—"

The SO keyed Boxer. "Skipper, target bearing forty five degrees . . . Range twenty five thousand yards . . . Speed one five knots."

"Roger that," Boxer answered.

"Could be the *African Star*?" Cowly asked.

"Could be," Boxer said with a nod. He was glad that something came along that changed the subject.

"Skipper, target going to a new heading," the SO said.

Boxer glanced at Cowly. "If it's her, she'll sail in box-like pattern at the rendezvous point."

"New course nine zero degrees," the SO said.

"ID?" Boxer asked.

"Should have come up on both our screens by now," the SO answered.

Boxer keyed the DCO. "The Ship's ID System isn't responding."

"Roger that . . . Will run a check," DCO answered.

Boxer scanned the COMCOMP. All operating systems were green. The *Turtle* would surface at the precise coordinates that Boxer had dialed into the AUTO-NAVSYS shortly after he had opened the sealed orders. They were one hundred feet down and traveling at twenty five knots. They'd reach the rendezvous point in less than forty minutes.

The DCO keyed Boxer. "SIDSYS functioning, Skipper, I played our test tapes into it. The target must be a new ship."

"Roger that," Boxer said and relayed the information to the SO.

"Well, we have a tape of her now," the SO answered.

Boxer switched on the NAVCLOCK.

"Any radio contact?" Cowly asked.

Boxer shook his head. He motioned to Lipner. "We'll be surfacing in thirty eight minutes. Fifteen minutes before we break water I'll alert the crew. I want all gun crews at their stations and the bow and stern deck details ready to take lines aboard."

"Aye, aye, Skipper," Lipner answered.

Boxer turned his attention to the COMCOMP. All operating systems continued to be green.

The SO keyed Boxer. "Target changing course again."

"Roger that," Boxer answered.

"If it's our ship," Cowly said, "she should come to course two seven zero."

Boxer switched on the Sonar screen. "That's what she's doing," he said.

Fifteen minutes before surfacing, a red warning light on the COMCOMP began to flash.

Boxer hit the klaxon twice; then he switched on the MC. "All systems are on AUTO . . . Surfacing will be done on AUTO . . . Section chiefs monitor your equipment . . . Commander Lowe to the bridge, on the double."

In less than two minutes Cynthia was on the bridge.

"I want you to watch the instrument readings," Boxer said. "So far everything is green."

"Aye, aye, Skipper," she answered.

Boxer looked at her and nodded.

She managed a thin smile.

Lipner switched on the MC. "All gun crews stand by . . . All gun crews stand by . . . Stations as soon as we surface . . . Gun crews to stations as soon as we surface . . . Forward and aft deck details stand by . . . Forward and aft deck details stand by topside to take lines aboard."

Boxer looked back at Lipner and gave him a thumbs up.

Lipner grinned broadly.

Boxer turned his attention to the COMCOMP. "Ballast should be venting about now," he said.

"There go the diving planes," Cynthia commented. "An easy zero three degrees."

"Ah, here's where everyone is!" Bush exclaimed,

coming onto the bridge. "And no one thought to invite me."

Ignoring the jibe, Boxer said over the MC, "Going to night lighting." The white lighting became red.

"Coming up to the red line," Cynthia said, watching the time to surface clock.

Boxer switched on the MC. "Four five seconds to surface and counting . . . All gun crews and deck details stand by."

The SO keyed Boxer. "Target will be one thousand yards off our bow . . . Bearing three six zero degrees . . . Speed one five knots."

"Roger that," Boxer said. He went back on the MC. "Fifteen seconds and counting . . . Stand by . . . Stand by." He pressed several buttons and changed three switch positions.

A bell began to ring and a green light flashed over the COMCOMP.

"Surface," Boxer announced. "Surface."

The deck and gun crews broke open the hatches and rushed to their respective places.

Boxer had elevated the gun turrets and bridge immediately prior to breaking water.

"Cowly," Boxer said, "take the CONN topside."

"Aye, aye, Skipper."

Boxer keyed the EO. "Reduce speed to zero eight knots."

"Reducing speed to zero eight knots."

Cowly keyed Boxer. "She's signaling with a flasher."

"Roger that," Boxer answered. He keyed the COMMO. "Send a signalman topside to the bridge."

"Aye, aye, Skipper," the COMMO answered.

"Lipner," Boxer said. "Secure the inside bridge. I'm going topside.

"Aye, aye, Skipper."

Boxer stood up, stretched and started to move away

from the COMCOMP.

"I thought you'd be in your quarters," Bush said to Cynthia.

"I was called to the bridge," she answered.

"Why wasn't I called to the bridge?" Bush asked.

"You weren't needed," Boxer answered.

"Just the chosen few, eh," Bush said with a smirk.

"I'll pretend I didn't hear that," Boxer said. "Do either of you wish to come topside with me?"

"I'll go," Cynthia said.

"So will I," Bush answered.

Boxer took the lead. He was on the bridge in less than fifteen seconds.

"It's the *African Star*," Cowly said.

"Did you ID us?" Boxer asked.

"Not yet."

Boxer turned to the signalman. "Send the word *Turtle*," he said.

"Aye, aye, Skipper," the signalman said and immediately began to flash out the letters of the word.

Within moments the *African Star* answered.

"Give it to us," Boxer told the signalman.

"Stand by to receive boarders . . . Approach on the port side . . . Heaving to now."

"Acknowledge that," Boxer told the signalman. He switched on the MC. "Mahony to the bridge, on the double."

Seconds later Mahony scrambled up through the open hatchway. "Reporting as ordered, Skipper."

"Take the helm and bring us on the portside of the *African Star*. I want to be close enough to allow us to be boarded."

"Aye, aye, Skipper," Mahony said.

Boxer switched off the AUTONAVSYS and then keyed the EO. "Go to zero five knots."

"Going to zero five knots," the EO answered.

Boxer keyed the RO. "What's the exact distance between us and the *African Star?*"

"Eight hundred yards and closing," the RO answered.

"Signal me when we reach two hundred yards," Boxer said.

"Aye, aye, Skipper," the RO answered.

Boxer took a few moments to look at the sea and the sky. The sea was calm and looked as if it were coated with silver. Half way down the zenith a white full moon illuminated the sky blotting out all but the brightest of stars. He turned his attention to the *African Star.*

"I'm going below," Bush announced; then to Cynthia, he said, "The party is dull up here. Care to join me for a better one?"

Boxer and Cowly exchanged glances.

"No thank you, Captain," Cynthia said.

"Some other time then," Bush said with a leer. "Some other time when you positively must have some action."

Boxer was about to say something, but the EO keyed him. "Coming up on two hundred yards, Skipper."

"Roger that," Boxer answered. He keyed the EO. "Twelve hundred rpms."

"Going to twelve hundred rpms," the EO answered.

The *Turtle* began to lose headway.

Boxer watched Mahony ease the wheel over.

The *Turtle* responded: her bow swinging to the portside of the *African Star* and then easing off to the starboard.

"Lined up, Skipper," Mahony said with evident satisfaction.

"Lined up," Boxer echoed. He waited a few seconds; then he keyed the EO. "Stop all engines."

"All engines stopped."

The *Turtle* continued to move forward. But with each passing second she lost her forward momentum. Finally she was alongside the *African Star.*

Boxer keyed the EO. "Reverse twelve hundred rpms

for thirty seconds."

"Reverse twelve hundred rpms for thirty seconds."

The *Turtle* shuddered and then was dead in the water.

"Stand by to take the line," an officer on the *African Star* said on a bull horn.

Boxer turned on the deck bow and stern lights.

The bow and stern lines were thrown down. Within moments the *Turtle* was lashed to the *African Star*.

"Stand by to receive boarders," the *African Star*'s deck officer said.

"Standing by," Boxer answered over the MC; then to Cowly, he said, "Take the CONN."

"Aye, aye, Skipper," Cowly answered.

Boxer dropped down the hatchway, hurried through the base of the bridge and through the open bulkhead door leading to the deck.

"Baggage coming aboard," the *African Star*'s officer said, as three large suitcases were lowered to the deck and were quickly picked up by members of the deck.

"Stand by for passengers," the ship's officer said.

The plural wasn't wasted on Boxer. He looked up and saw two men carefully working their way down the ship's ladder. The smaller of the two was Sanchez, but he didn't have any idea who the other man was.

As soon as Sanchez reached the deck of the *Turtle*, Boxer went to him and said, "Welcome aboard Julio."

Sanchez turned and crossing himself, he said in Spanish, "Mother of God what this poor sinner has to do."

Boxer grinned at him.

"Grin," Sanchez said, "but even you wouldn't enjoy coming down that excuse for a staircase." Then he seized Boxer's hand, shook it vigorously, embraced and kissing him on both cheeks, he asked, "And how are you, old friend?"

"Fine. And you?" Boxer asked.

"Excellent!" Sanchez answered, using the Spanish pronunciation, instead of the English.

Finally, the other man stepped down on the deck. He had the build of a small size sumo wrestler. He was sweating profusely and wiped his face with a handkerchief.

Sanchez turned to him. "I told you it would be fun and games as soon as we left the *African Star*." Then to Boxer he said, "Captain Boxer, permit me to introduce Mister Bruno Morell . . . Used to be Morellie, but Morell is a better name in the Company."

"Welcome aboard Mr. Morell," Boxer said, shaking the man's hand, which was easily twice the size of his.

"My pleasure," Mr. Morell answered in a pleasant voice. "But please call me Bruno . . . everyone does."

Boxer looked around at the gun crews; all of them were in position.

"This is a sub?" Sanchez asked.

"It's a submarine alright," Boxer said. "You'll see that in a matter of minutes. Let's get below. I want to get underway as soon as possible."

"Lead the way," Sanchez answered.

"Through that door," Boxer said, gesturing toward the open bulkhead door and at the same time wondering whether Morell would make it through the hatchways.

As soon as they were inside Boxer directed them to the bridge. "As you can see," he said, "the seating accommodations are not the best. I'd take you topside, but as soon as we cast off, we'll dive again."

"Do what you have to do," Sanchez said.

Boxer nodded and keyed Cowly. "Cast off and take her down to six zero feet."

"Aye, aye, Skipper," Cowly answered.

A moment later Cowly's voice came over the MC. He ordered the fore and aft lines cast off. Then he said, "All hands clear the deck . . . All hands clear the deck . . .

Prepare to dive . . . Prepare to dive!"

A shudder passed through the *Turtle* as the propellers began grabbing water.

"We're underway," Boxer announced.

The Chief of the deck detail keyed Boxer. "Skipper, where do you want the suitcases put?"

"I'll tell you in a minute," Boxer answered and he asked Sanchez and Bruno if they would mind sharing a cabin together.

"No," Sanchez said.

Boxer looked at Bruno.

"It's okay with me," he answered.

Boxer keyed the Chief and told him to put the suitcases in Mr. Cowly's quarters. "Then stand by to move Mr. Cowly's gear into Captain Bush's cabin.

"Aye, aye, Skipper," the Chief answered.

Suddenly there were three short blasts on the klaxon.

"Holy shit, what a sound!" Bruno exclaimed.

"Dive," Cowly said over the MC. "Dive . . . Dive!"

The bridge detail came down through the hatchway and rushed to their stations.

Cowly took his place at the COMCOMP and adjusted several dials and switches.

"Lower bridge," Cowly told his acting EXO.

"Aye, aye," the man answered. "Bridge being lowered."

Cowly keyed the DO. "Make six zero feet."

"Aye, aye," the DO answered.

Cowly ran a systems check. "All systems green," he announced over the MC. Then he turned to Boxer and asked, "What's our new heading, Skipper?"

"Use the coordinates of our objective for now," Boxer answered.

"Aye, aye," Cowly said and turning back to the COMCOMP, he set a new latitude and longitude into AUTONAVSYS and NAVCLOCK.

Boxer suddenly realized that Cynthia was standing off to one side. "Commander Lowe," he said, "I'd like you to meet these two gentlemen: Mr. Sanchez and Mr. Morell."

Cynthia smiled and shook their hands.

Boxer introduced them to Cowly and the other officers on the bridge. Then he said, "I'll put you in Commander Lowe's hands for the next few hours. She'll see that you're properly clothed, and she's the best person aboard to give you an overall tour of the *Turtle.*"

"We're in your hands, Commander," Sanchez said with a smile.

"I think we'll get you clothed first," Cynthia said and led them off to the supply room.

Boxer waited until the three of them were off the bridge before he told Cowly that he'd be bunking with Bush.

"He's not going to like it," Cowly said.

Boxer shrugged. "I don't have any other place to put them."

"I'm not sure I like it either," Cowly said.

"I didn't think you would," Boxer answered. "But it will make it easier for you to monitor him."

"He's not a fool, Skipper. He's going to tumble to what I'm doing."

"Probably. But something is very wrong with him and I'd like to be able to—"

"Relieve him from duty before he does real damage," Cowly said.

"Something like that," Boxer responded.

This time Cowly shrugged. "That's a long shot, Skipper."

"It's the only shot I have," Boxer said.

The DO keyed Cowly. "Coming to six zero feet."

"Roger that," Cowly answered, checking the DDRO and then the depth gauge.

"Trimming," the DO said.

"Roger that," Cowly responded.

"I'll be in my quarters," Boxer said. He looked at the digital clock. It was 03:45:14. "I want every officer in the mess area at zero eight hundred."

"Aye, aye, Skipper."

"It's time to tell the men where they're going and what they're expected to do," Boxer said.

"I thought that Sanchez was the only one coming aboard," Cowly commented.

"So did I," Boxer said.

"Then why is Morell—I mean Bruno—here?"

"I haven't asked," Boxer said. "But you can be sure that I will soon be told." Then he added, "That's the fun of working with Sanchez, you never know which rabbit he's going to pull from which hat, or if there are any rabbits, or for that matter any hats. See you in a few hours."

With a smile, Cowly answered, "See you."

Fourteen

Boxer moved to the front of the mess area. Every officer aboard the *Turtle* was present. "I'll make this as brief as possible. With the exception of my EXO, Major Vargas and Captain Bush, all of you have been wondering about this particular shake-down cruise. If I were in your shoes, I'd be wondering too. This *is* a shake-down cruise, but it is also a mission. We're going to land on the Libyan coast, attack a prison camp and rescue prisoners."

A stunned silence filled the room.

Boxer went on. "We don't have time for practice runs. We have to get it right the first time. I'm not going to ask for questions at this time; as soon as I know more, you will know more.

"Cowly, Bush and Vargas report to my quarters. The rest of you are dismissed."

Bush came up to Boxer. "You hit them hard, Skipper."

Boxer nodded. "If there was another way to do it, I would have."

"They're waiting for the other shoe to fall."

"So am I," Boxer said. "That's why we're going to my quarters. Sanchez and Bruno hold the other shoe."

"I guessed that," Bush answered, falling in alongside Boxer as he started to walk.

Boxer had expected Bush to be difficult about sharing his quarters with Cowly. But he wasn't and Boxer was, as the expression goes, thankful for small favors.

Boxer's cabin was crowded. Bruno and Sanchez sat on the bunk. Boxer was at his desk. Bush occupied the chair. Without keeping the door open, there wasn't any room to put two additional chairs for Cowly and Vargas.

"The purpose of this meeting," Boxer said, "is to find out about our objective from the man who is going to lead us there, Mr. Sanchez."

Sanchez smiled and held up his hand. "You give me too much credit," he said, "or the balls I don't have. Bruno will lead you. Not forty eight hours ago, he left the camp."

Boxer had guessed that Bruno's presence had meant something, but he would have never guessed that he would be the point man.

"I'll let him tell you about your objective," Sanchez said. "Bruno, it's all yours."

"Well, gents," Bruno said, "I don't really know where to begin. I guess the first thing you should know is that the camp is not only a prison camp but it's also a training camp for the Sushas, an extremist Arab group."

Vargas glanced at Boxer.

"There are always some five hundred of them in residence, so to speak," Bruno said.

"All we can see from the recon photographs," Boxer said, "is a few scattered tents on the crest of a small hill."

"That's not the camp," Bruno said. "The camp is ten kilometers to the east of that. That's a radar station which we will destroy. The heart of the camp is a series of caves located in a giant outcropping of rock. The prisoners are kept in those caves."

"How the hell are we going to get into the caves," Vargas asked, "and come out alive?"

"Good question," Bruno responded. "The caves are linked to an ancient Roman fortress above them by a series of tunnels. The Romans were great builders," he commented appreciatively.

"That still doesn't tell us how we're going to do it," Cowly said.

"The Sushas don't bother with the fortress," Bruno said, "and even their commander doesn't know about the tunnels. One of the tunnels runs alongside the chamber where the prisoners are kept. All that separates them is a two foot rock wall which we can blast open."

"That means two strike forces," Vargas said. "One coming at them from the front, and the second hitting them from behind."

"Three," Bruno said. "The third will blow the radar station."

"And while we're doing all this," Boxer asked, "what will the Sushas be doing?"

"Fighting," Bruno said.

"And so will all of the Libyan forces," Bush commented. "They'll be fighting *us*."

"Some of them no doubt will," Bruno answered.

"That gives us about a ten percent chance of getting out," Vargas said.

"I'd say about twenty-five percent," Bruno said coolly.

"I sure as hell don't like those odds," Vargas told him frankly.

"They are what they are," Bruno answered.

"How much time do we have to complete the mission ashore?" Boxer asked.

"No more than two hours."

"When do we go?"

"Between oh one hundred and oh three hundred," Bruno answered.

"What happens if we're discovered before we hit the camp?" Bush asked.

"Our chances for success and survival drop to around five percent," Bruno answered.

"What casualty rate can we expect?" Cowly asked.

"Seventy-five percent of the assault force."

Boxer gave a long low whistle.

"You can say that again, Skipper," Vargas said.

"That's steep," Boxer told him.

"That's going to be the price," Bruno answered defensively.

"Let's assume that we get in and out of the camp," Boxer said, "and we make our way back to the boat. Then we're going to have to fight our way to the open sea."

"Only out of the gulf," Sanchez said.

"Why that boundary?"

"Because a carrier group will be there to defend you should you need to be defended. I have the necessary coded message that you will send the moment we leave."

"That means we'll have to make a two hundred mile dash, and hope that we can reach the carrier group before the Libyans can reach us," Cowly said.

"It's the best cover that could be given to us," Sanchez answered.

"What about the beach where we—"

"A cove—one of the few on the coast," Bruno said. "If we had to go ashore some other place you'd have a very strong current to contend with. But this cove is five hundred yards across and the beach has a good slope to it. You'll be able to land your men and your equipment about twenty yards out."

"What's the depth there?"

"Thirty feet."

"That doesn't put much water between us and the surface," Cowly said.

"What's the maximum depth in the cove?"

"Ninety feet," Bruno answered. "But once you're out of the cove, the bottom drops off to one hundred fifty feet."

"The *Turtle* could wait outside the cove and come in again just before the men return," Bush suggested.

"I wouldn't want to risk having something go wrong," Boxer said. "We'll stand by and wait on the beach."

"Anything else?" Bruno asked.

"I need a complete layout of the area," Vargas said, "in order to make maps."

"That's no problem. I'll even be able to give you details on their defensive positions."

"On their what?" Boxer asked.

"Where they have their cannon placed."

"Rocket launchers?"

"Only two."

"Christ," Cowly said, "this goes from bad to worse."

"You didn't expect that camp to be—"

"A death trap," Bush said, finishing the sentence.

"With careful planning and the element of surprise on our side," Bruno said doggedly, "the mission can be accomplished."

Everyone in the room was silent until Boxer said, "We have two more tests to run on the sea trials before we begin the mission. We have a deep dive and an undersea movement involving the use of the *Turtle*'s treads."

"How long will those tests take?" Bruno asked.

"The deep dive about twelve hours and the other not more than three or four. For each of them I have to find a particular place in the ocean. The deep dive can take place off the south of France in the Mediterranean, and the other test could be made somewhere off Corsica."

"How long would it take us to get to the test sights?" Sanchez asked.

Boxer turned to the COMCOMP and typed in the *Turtle*'s present latitude and longitude. Then he asked for a map display of the western Mediterranean, chose two sets of coordinates, and typed them into the COMCOMP. Using an average speed of twenty-five knots, he asked the COMCOMP to compute the time it would take to go from where *Turtle* was to the first set of coordinates; then from

200

there to the second set.

The answer: forty-four hours, thirty-one minutes came up on the screen and was immediately followed by a second answer of four hours and three minutes.

"We're talking of about sixty hours," Bruno said.

"That's about right," Boxer answered.

"The run between the last test sight and the landing point is probably eight hours at the most."

Boxer nodded.

Bruno moved his eyes from man to man; then he said, "I have the necessary topographical information to give the mission a good chance of success."

"Gentlemen," Boxer said, "there's no question about the danger involved. Your job will be to minimize it . . . Spic, parley with Bruno; I want an operations plan from you within the next thirty-six hours."

"Aye, aye, Skipper," Vargas answered.

"Bush, you do the same. I want to have more than a damn good idea what that cove is all about before I get there."

"Aye, aye, Skipper," Bush replied.

"Cowly, I want you to work out two alternate landing and departure sites with Bruno," Boxer said.

"Aye, aye, Skipper," Cowly responded.

"Alright, gentlemen, our next meeting will be thirty-six hours from now. Any questions?"

"I have one," Bush said.

"Okay, let's have it."

"What will our epitaph read? I hope it will be something inspiring like 'Those of you who died were fools for attempting the impossible.'"

"That's not funny, Captain," Boxer said tersely.

"Sorry, Skipper. I thought this whole meeting funny. Not funny ha ha, but funny like the Sunday funnies."

Boxer could feel the color come into his cheeks. He had it within his power to relieve Bush of any responsibility during the mission. But that was a drastic step which he preferred to avoid taking.

"Skipper," Vargas said, "Captain Bush was only saying aloud what all of us must be thinking to ourselves."

Boxer took a deep breath and slowly exhaled. "I don't like the mission anymore than you do, but there's nothing I can do about it."

"Sorry, Skipper," Bush said, "there is something you can do: you can radio Headquarters and tell them what Bruno told us."

"They already know it," Bruno said. "I spoke with Mr. Kinkade and Admiral Stark when I was aboard the *African Star*."

"We go," Boxer said definitively.

As the men filed out of Boxer's room, he said, "Julio, stay for a few minutes."

"At your service, Skipper," Sanchez answered, moving back into the room.

"Close the door and sit down," Boxer said.

"Not an easy session for you, eh, Skipper?"

"That's because it's not going to be easy for them later on," Boxer answered. "The odds on this one are shorter than some of the others we've been on."

"Bruno—"

Boxer held up his hand. "I didn't ask you to stay, Julio, to discuss the mission. I wanted to thank you for finding the bastards who killed my mother."

Sanchez smiled broadly. "I heard you handled it beautifully. My men were very impressed with you."

"And I was very impressed with them," Boxer said.

"If you ever quit this racket," Sanchez said, "you can always work for me."

"Thanks, I'll remember that," Boxer answered. "Now

I have two questions—no, three questions."

"What's the first?"

"Who and what is Bruno Morell?"

"I already told you."

"Not good enough. This mission is too fucking risky to go with more unknowns than I have to."

"Okay, he's one of your boys—but he sometimes works for me."

"Who's he working for now?"

"Half your people and half me."

"What's in it for you?" Boxer asked.

"I can't tell you that, Skipper," Sanchez said with a smile.

Boxer knew that it was useless to push Sanchez. "Okay," he said, "second question: Why are the prisoners suddenly so important that they have to be rescued now. This camp has been there for a while, hasn't it?"

"The camp has been there for a while," Sanchez answered, "but some of the prisoners are recent arrivals. That's about as much as I'm going to tell you."

"Then the Sushas have someone in there that is important to us?"

"You said you had three questions," Sanchez said.

Boxer nodded. "Why couldn't we ID the *African Star*?"

Sanchez smiled broadly. "Because we changed the sound of the drive shaft."

"You did what?"

"Changed the sound of the drive shaft." Sanchez said. "It's really very easy . . . We took the original sound, fed it into some kind of electronic device and then fed the new sound into underwater speakers . . . That's what your equipment picked up."

"Terrific," Boxer exclaimed.

"Sure it is," Sanchez said enthusiastically. "It'll drive the Russians nuts until they figure out how to pick up the primary frequency."

"Kinkade knows about it?" Boxer asked.

Sanchez nodded. "Part of the money to develop it came from the Company."

"I might have guessed," Boxer said sarcastically.

"Listen," Sanchez said, "I always give value for what I'm paid."

"So you do," Boxer said. "So you do."

"By the way, what's eating Captain Bush?"

Boxer shook his head. "I don't know."

"He's trouble," Sanchez said. "Believe me, Skipper, I know all the signs. The man is trouble."

"I hope not," Boxer said. "When we hit that beach we're going to have enough trouble staying alive."

"Maybe it won't be as bad as you think," Sanchez suggested.

"You can bet," Boxer said, "it's going to be worse— much worse."

Sanchez raised his eyebrows.

"Intuition," Boxer said. "Intuition."

Trish answered the phone.

"I would like to speak to Comrade Captain Boxer," a man with a thick eastern European accent said.

"Who is this?" Trish asked.

"Comrade Captain Borodine," the man replied.

"You can't be!" Trish exclaimed. "Now whoever you are stop joking around."

"I am not, as you put it, 'joking around.' I have just come from Moscow and I wish to speak with my friend."

Trish's brow furrowed. "He is not here now," she answered.

"Then would you be so kind as to tell him that I phoned and I will phone again," Borodine said.

Trish started to say that she would give Boxer the

message, but she stopped herself and instead she told Borodine that if he would come to the apartment, he would be able to meet him when he returned.

"A cafe . . . I mean a cocktail lounge would be better," Borodine said.

"There's a lovely one on the Potomac. It's called Lucy's Place. Can you meet us there?"

"Yes. Are you Trish?"

"Yes, but how did you know my name?" she asked.

"Comrade Captain Boxer told me all about you," Borodine answered.

"I really hope not all," Trish said.

Borodine laughed and said, "I am looking forward to meeting you."

Trish looked at her watch. It was three thirty in the afternoon. "Could you be at Lucy's Place in an hour?" she asked.

"That would be no trouble," Borodine answered.

Trish put the phone down and smiled happily . . . This time she'd be able to surprise the hell out of Jack. The idea of having drinks with Borodine thrilled her.

Suddenly she panicked. How would she recognize Borodine? She had never seen him, or even a picture of him. She had absolutely no idea what he looked like.

Then just as quickly she calmed down. Borodine would be easy to spot. "He'd be the man who'd look more out of place at the bar than any other man," she said aloud.

Pleased with herself, Trish was looking forward to the adventure of meeting the famous Comrade Captain Igor Borodine. Though Boxer seldom spoke about what he did, or whom he did it with, she knew from what little he said that Borodine was one of the few men he truly respected and Julio Sanchez was the other.

Trish dressed carefully for her cocktail meeting. She chose a black dress with just a low enough neckline to reveal the tops of her breasts, which were as deeply

205

tanned as the rest of her. A single strand of pearls decorated her neck and her hair was swept up in a bun. She wore high-heeled shoes, and, because it was very hot in Washington, no stockings.

When she was finished dressing, Trish appraised herself in the bedroom mirror. "Chic and sexy," she said aloud, "or should it be sexy and chic?" She laughed, and moments later she was on her way to meet Borodine.

Lucy's Place had once been a working barge, but it had been drastically altered into its present state. It was moored close to a Marina and its huge blue tinted glass windows overlooked the river on three sides. Inside, it was tastefully decorated in a nautical motif, with fishnets, huge oars and a variety of other paraphernalia related to the sea. The bar was shaped like a huge harp made of darkly stained oak. Behind it was an enormous, multi-partitioned, exquisitely landscaped fish tank with scores of vividly colored tropical fish.

Lucy's Place was one of the few cocktail lounges in Washington that her grandfather truly enjoyed visiting.

Glad to be out of the steamy late afternoon, Trish entered the cool, wood panelled foyer and decided to make a stop in the powder room before entering the bar. She carefully examined her face and wherever she saw a shiny spot she eliminated it with a deft application of powder. Well, she thought, as the old expression goes: "You look good enough to eat."

Trish left the powder room, reentered the foyer and, with her heart pounding, she walked into the already crowded bar where the late afternoon sun was streaming through the large blue-tinted windows.

It took a few moments before her eyes became accustomed to the lighting. Then she looked toward the bar. Many men and women were seated on high back

206

stools or standing, with drinks in their hands, close by the bar.

Though many of the men eyed her, some no doubt thinking she was a prostitute, none of them looked the way Trish thought Borodine should look. She moved deeper into the room. All of the small, round, candle lit cocktail tables were occupied. She considered going to the bar and ordering a drink, but the thought of having to fend off or ignore various offers of drinks and dinner did not appeal to her.

Suddenly the hostess came straight toward her. "Are you Mrs. McElroy?" she asked.

"Yes," Trish answered, her heart beginning to pound again.

"Would you please follow me, Mrs. McElroy," the hostess said. "Your friend is waiting for you."

Trish nodded.

The hostess led her across the room to one of the tables close to the window.

Borodine stood up. He was dressed in a tan, American-cut, poplin summer suit, a white shirt and dark brown tie. Though he was dressed similarly to the other men in the room, there was an indefinable difference about him. For one thing, he could have been Jack's brother, or at least a first cousin. Except for the fact that Borodine was shorter than Jack by at least a good two inches, the resemblance between them was startling.

Trish smiled at him.

Borodine took hold of her hand and kissed the back of it. "It is a pleasure to meet you. But where is Comrade Captain Boxer?" he asked.

"I'll tell you all about it," Trish said. "But first I must have a drink."

Borodine gestured to the chair and said, "Please sit down."

"What are you drinking?" Trish asked.

"Vodka," he answered.

"That's it, just vodka?"

He nodded.

"Oh well, I'll have a screwdriver," Trish said. "That's vodka and orange juice."

Borodine smiled and summoned the waitress. "A screwdriver for the lady and another vodka for me," he said.

"And would you please bring us two large plates of those delicious hors d'oeuvres."

"Now tell me where is my friend," Borodine said.

"First you must tell me how you recognized me?" Trish asked.

"Comrade Captain Boxer showed me your picture," Borodine said.

Trish smiled. "And you remembered?"

"A beautiful woman is easy to remember," Borodine said.

"Would you mind if I smoked?" Trish asked.

Borodine shook his head. "I would not mind. But it is not good for you."

"Do you smoke?"

Borodine nodded.

"It is not good for you either," Trish said. "But you do it."

Borodine reached into the inside breast pocket of his jacket and withdrew a hard pack of cigarettes. He gave her one; then struck a match and held it for her. "Now you must tell me—"

"He's away," she answered, sitting upright again; then she quickly added, "But I wanted to meet you."

Borodine was about to ask why, when the waitress returned with their drinks and hors d'oeuvres.

"Will you be here long?" Trish asked.

"Several months," Borodine answered. "I am an advisor to our negotiators at the arms reduction conferences."

"Sounds important," Trish said.

Borodine shrugged.

"But you'd rather be at sea, wouldn't you?"

"At this moment, my dear Mrs. McElroy, I'd rather be right here with you," Borodine said, as he lifted his glass. "To Comrade Captain Boxer," he toasted.

Trish touched her glass to his. "To Captain Boxer," she said.

They drank.

"Eat some of these goodies," Trish said, putting down her glass and helping herself to a baked clam.

"Will I be able to meet my friend tomorrow evening," Borodine asked.

Trish shook her head. "Not for two or three weeks, I'm afraid."

Borodine picked up a cracker with lobster salad.

"You know," she told him, "I often wondered what you were like. Not only what you looked like, but what kind of a man you were. Jack, though he has spoken about you often, never said much about—"

"And what kind of man do you find me?" Borodine asked, after he had taken another swallow of vodka.

"Charming," Trish said with a smile.

"And nothing more?"

"Rather handsome and somewhat mysterious."

"Mysterious?" Borodine questioned, helping himself to a cracker topped with red caviar.

Trish nodded. "The way Jack is mysterious," she said. "A woman looks at you and knows that there's something about you that's different from the other men she sees. It's . . . it's an aura about you." She lifted her drink and took several sips of it before she put it down.

Borodine looked out at the river. Many of the small boats that had been out for a day's sailing were returning to the marina.

"Is there anything like this in Russia?" Trish asked.

Borodine shook his head. "Our economy would not

support it," he answered, facing Trish again.

Suddenly she realized he was looking at her breasts. The expression on his face told her what he was thinking. "I would like another drink," she said.

"Good idea!" Borodine exclaimed, looking around for the waitress.

"Jack told me about the loss of your wife and child," Trish said.

"I try not to think about it," Borodine responded. "It makes it easier that way."

Trish nodded understandingly.

"Ah, the waitress is coming," Borodine said, helping himself to a cigarette and lighting it.

"Jack will be very pleased to see you," Trish said.

"He is a unique man," Borodine told her, just as the waitress came to the table.

"Do it again," Trish said.

"Is that the expression you use to order a second drink?"

"Yes, if you want to drink the same thing."

Borodine nodded and took a drag on the cigarette. "Did you know he saved my entire crew?"

Trish shook her head. "He said nothing about it."

Borodine smiled. "A unique man, your Comrade Captain Boxer," he commented, taking another drag on the cigarette.

"Oh my God!" Trish exclaimed.

"What's wrong?" Borodine asked.

"My ex-husband has just entered the room and has seen me. He's coming to the table."

Borodine turned his attention to the tall, dignified looking man walking toward them. McElroy was physically a very different kind of a man from Boxer.

"Well, Trish," McElroy said, "I didn't expect to see you here and with a new friend. What happened to the famous Captain Jack Boxer?"

210

"Jack is away," Trish answered.

"Ah, so his mouse will play," McElroy commented, looking at Borodine. "This one looks a lot like—"

"Comrade Captain Borodine," Trish said, "my ex-husband John McElroy."

Borodine started to stand.

"A Russian. You're sitting here having cocktails with a Russian Captain!" McElroy exclaimed, his voice becoming louder and louder.

"John, stop it," Trish said.

"This man is a killer. This man is our avowed enemy," McElroy shouted.

Everyone in the room and at the bar turned toward McElroy.

"John—"

"Killer," McElroy shouted, pointing at Borodine. "This Russian has killed Americans. Look at him people! He looks like any other man here but he's not . . . he's commander of—"

Borodine was on his feet. His fist smashed into McElroy's jaw, knocking him to the floor.

"Let's get out of here," Trish said.

"I have to pay for the drinks," Borodine told her.

"Ten dollars would be more than enough," Trish said.

Borodine dropped ten dollars on the table.

Trish took hold of his hand. "Let's go," she said and dragged him toward the door.

"That man is crazy!" Borodine exclaimed. "He could have caused a riot."

"He would have liked nothing better," Trish said, still holding on to his hand. "That's the way he is." She led him along a walkway that was close to the river. She was breathing very rapidly. "John will make sure that the whole incident will be in the morning papers. I'm sorry, Igor . . . I really am."

He stopped, swung her toward him and kissed her hard

on the lips.

She opened her mouth and put her arms around him. She needed someone to hold her, to make love to her.

"This is what I wanted to do almost from the first moment I saw you," Igor said.

Trish drew away from him. "Let's walk," she said.

Borodine nodded.

For several minutes they walked without speaking to each other. Then Trish asked, "Are you sure you want to go to bed with me?"

"Are you sure?" Borodine asked,

She shook her head. "I am not sure of anything right now. I can't think straight. You decide. I'll do whatever you decide."

Taking hold of her hand again, Borodine started to walk.

"What did you decide?" Trish asked after another long silence.

"To take you to dinner," Borodine said, looking at her.

She uttered a deep sigh; the danger was over.

"This will be our secret," Borodine commented. "We will always know that the opportunity and the willingness were there, and we turned away from it."

Trish raised his hand to her lips and kissed it. "Neither one of us would have been happy afterwards," she said.

"And neither one of us is completely happy now," Borodine answered.

Trish smiled. "Fidelity and loyalty have their price," she said, "and we're paying it."

"What would you like to eat?" Borodine asked, changing the subject.

Fifteen

Boxer keyed the DO. "Make one thousand feet."

"Making one thousand feet," the DO responded.

Boxer ran SYSCHEK. All systems were green.

"Passing through two zero zero feet," the DO announced.

"Roger that," Boxer answered, as the same numbers came up on the DDRO and the depth gauge above the COMCOMP.

"What would you do if the numbers didn't check out?" Cynthia asked softly. She was standing to Boxer's left. Cowly was at his regular duty station and Bush was to Boxer's right.

Bush answered, "We'd stop the dive and run DSYSCHK and if we couldn't come up with a correction, the dive would be aborted, unless, of course, we were in a combat situation."

"DPLANES going to one zero degrees," the DO reported.

"Roger that," Boxer said, as he watched the Diving Plane Inclinator move from zero degrees to ten degrees.

The *Turtle*'s bow dipped forward and her rate of descent accelerated.

"Passing through three zero zero feet," the DO said.

"Roger that," Boxer answered.

"Between three hundred and three hundred and fifty

213

feet," Cynthia said, "the liquid plastic starts to become a solid. The solidification process is complete by the time four hundred feet is reached."

Boxer glanced at her and nodded.

She leaned slightly forward and pointed to a dial. "The needle has already begun to move. It's calibrated in NIGS; each NIG is a degree of hardness. With the needle at zero the plastic has the consistency and appearance of petroleum jelly."

"Passing through four hundred feet," the DO reported.

"Roger that," Boxer answered.

"The needle has moved to NIG ten; the solidification is complete."

"How thick is the coating?" Boxer asked.

"Only a half inch thick . . . But put down very precisely . . . From place to place it doesn't vary more than plus or minus ten thousandths of an inch."

"And it will solidify the same way if struck by a shell or a missile?" Bush asked.

"Yes, but under those conditions the molecular strain is enormous and it will not return to its liquid, or jelly state if you will, quickly and when it does, it could develop lumps."

"Passing through five zero zero feet," the DO said.

"Roger that," Boxer answered. "Stand by to go to AUTODIVSYS."

"Standing by to go to AUTODIVSYS," he told the DO.

"Ten four," the DO answered. "All systems green."

"Roger that," Boxer said.

"When does the solid begin to change back to its surface state?" Bush asked.

"At about the same depth that it becomes a solid," Cynthia said.

Boxer switched on the MC. "Passing through six zero

zero feet . . . We are on AUTODIVSYS control."

"Looking good," Cowly commented.

"Couldn't look any better," Boxer said.

Cynthia smiled.

"You look like the cat that just swallowed the canary," Boxer said.

"I feel like it," she answered.

"What does it take to get you to feel something else?" Bush asked.

The smile left Cynthia's face.

Boxer glanced at Bush. The man's face was taut with anger. The change was almost instantaneous.

"What would happen," Bush asked in a tight voice, "if the solid failed to liquify?"

"That's impossible," Cynthia answered, her voice just as tight as his.

Boxer looked at the DDRO. "Passing through seven five zero feet," he announced.

"Nothing is impossible," Bush said.

"That is impossible," Cynthia replied.

Aware of what was happening between Cynthia and Bush, Boxer was just about to tell Bush to leave the bridge when a red light began to flash on the COMCOMP and a warning siren sounded.

Boxer switched on the MC. "We have an emergency . . . All hands stand by . . . We have an emergency." He made SYSCHK . . . All systems were green. He keyed the DO. "Switching MANCONT . . . Bring her level."

"Aye, aye, Skipper," the DO answered.

The DCO keyed Boxer. "Skipper, the drive shaft seal opened . . . We're taking water in the drive shaft compartment . . . Activating high pressure pumps."

"Can we deal with it?" Boxer asked.

"Not if we go any deeper," the DCO said.

"Roger that," Boxer answered. He switched on the MC

again. "We have a ruptured drive shaft seal . . . We are taking on water but will soon have it under control . . . The test dive is terminated . . . I repeat the test dive is terminated."

The DCO keyed Boxer. "Skipper, I am inserting high pressure air into the shaft compartment. It will reinforce the seal from the inside."

"Roger that," Boxer answered and added, "Good thinking."

"Ten four," the DCO answered.

The DO keyed Boxer. "Boat level," he said.

"Roger that," Boxer answered, checking the null on the ELI and the bubble indicator.

Boxer ran SYSCHK. All systems were green. He keyed the DO. "Make one hundred feet. Easy."

"Making one hundred feet . . . easy," the DO answered.

"Better make design changes on those seals," he said to Cynthia.

"According to the specs they should have been good for two thousand feet," she answered.

"That one wasn't" he said succinctly.

The DCO keyed Boxer. "Skipper, I'd like to send my men out to look at that seal when we surface."

"They'll have to do it under water," Boxer answered.

"I'll need a minimum depth," the DCO told him.

"Roger that," Boxer answered.

"That could have been a real problem," Bush commented.

Boxer glared at him. "Captain, it is a real problem. It limits our operational ability. We can't dive to a depth where we might be relatively safe from attack."

Bush flushed.

Boxer keyed the DCO. "I can give you three zero feet."

"Ten four," the DCO answered.

Boxer keyed the DO. "Make three zero feet."

"Aye, aye, Skipper . . . Making three zero feet."

Boxer was doubly pissed. He was pissed at Bush before the seal failed, and pissed that the seal had ruptured.

"Skipper," Cowly said, "it's fourteen hundred hours. At three zero feet we'll be seen by any ship in the area and by any aircraft. The sea is very clear here."

Boxer nodded. "If we delay going to three zero feet," he said, "we might as well surface at night . . . Say about oh two hundred hours."

"I'd say that would be about right," Cowly replied.

Boxer keyed the DCO and the DO at the same time and gave them the change of plans. Then he said to the DO. "Make two zero zero feet and bring her level."

"Making two zero zero feet," the DO answered.

Boxer turned to Cowly. "Take the CONN." Then looking straight at Bush, he said, "In my quarters, Captain. . . . Now!"

Bush gave him a questioning look, nodded, turned and walked away.

"I'm going to settle this thing between you," Boxer said to Cynthia, "before it really gets in the way."

She nodded and said, "Do you want me present?"

"Yes," Boxer answered. "Yes. Then everything would be up front."

Boxer was at his desk. The MINICOMCOMP was switched on. Bush was seated on the bunk and Cynthia had the chair.

Boxer wasn't about to mince words. He glared straight at Bush. "Do you want to tell me what's going on," he asked.

"I don't know what you're talking about," Bush answered.

"Okay, I'll lay it out for you. You have been making sexual advances to Commander Lowe, which she finds repugnant and so do I."

Bush looked confused.

"And your comments on other occasions about our mission show an enormous lack of consideration for your fellow officers."

"I have no idea what you're talking about," Bush said.

Boxer looked at Cynthia. "Would you repeat some of the things Captain Bush said to you?"

"Allegedly said," Bush said.

"Allegedly said," Boxer repeated.

"On one occasion he came into my cabin on the pretext of wanting to ask a technical question and said, 'I dreamt about you last night.' I asked him to leave. He said, 'We were frenching one another.' Then he left. On another occasion, he said, 'I want to fuck you.'"

"Have you anything to say about these allegations, Captain?" Boxer asked.

"They are just that—allegations and nothing more."

"Both myself and Mr. Cowly have been present when you made direct sexual references to Commander Lowe," Boxer said.

Bush shook his head. "Skipper, I swear that I have nothing but the highest respect for Commander Lowe. I would not make any comments that would in any manner be insulting to her."

"But you did," Cynthia said. "Just before the seal failed you were—"

"Captain," Boxer said, "would you please wait outside the cabin for a few minutes."

"Aye, aye, Skipper," Bush answered, standing up and walked to the door. Then suddenly he stopped, turned around and said, "Ask her what she's been doing. Ask her about the way she wiggles her ass every time she passes me, or how she stretches so I can see her tits. Ask how she's been asking for it!"

Boxer was too surprised to respond.

Bush faced the door, opened it and walked into the passageway.

"My God," Cynthia exclaimed, "what the hell is going on with him?"

Boxer keyed the MO. "My quarters on the double."

"Aye, aye, Skipper," the MO answered.

Cynthia repeated her question.

"We'll wait for the MO," Boxer told her.

"His voice was different; even his face changed," Cynthia said.

Boxer nodded.

The MO arrived and closed the door behind him. "Captain Bush said Commander Lowe needed medical attention," he said.

"Sit down doc," Boxer said.

"But you don't look as if you're ill," the MO commented to Cynthia.

"She's not. But Captain Bush is," Boxer said. "I want you to listen to what Commander Lowe tells you. Some of it I heard and some Mr. Cowly heard. Commander Lowe, please tell the doc what you told me."

Cynthia told the doc about Bush's advances.

"But that's totally out of character," the MO said. "He's probably one of the most polite men I have ever met."

Boxer nodded and went on to explain how Bush acted at the briefing session.

The MO shook his head.

"Can you give me an idea of what is happening?" Boxer asked.

"I'm not really qualified to do that," the MO answered.

"What's your best guess?" Boxer asked.

"I don't want to guess—"

The DO keyed Boxer. "Coming to two zero zero feet and trimming."

"Roger that," Boxer said, checking the null on the MINICOMCOMP. He keyed Cowly. "Move in a square five by five miles."

"Aye, aye, Skipper," Cowly answered.

Boxer turned his attention back to the MO. "You were saying?"

"What you describe are the behavior characteristics of a schizoid. Before a person falls into that category, however, there are a great many other—"

Suddenly the MC was switched on. "Now hear this . . . Now hear this . . . This is Captain Bligh speaking."

"That's Bush!" Boxer exclaimed, leaping out of his chair. He keyed Cowly.

Cowly didn't answer.

"All hands, now hear this," Bush said. "I now command the *Turtle* . . . The *Turtle* is now under the command of Captain Bligh."

Boxer keyed Vargas. "Stand by with a half a dozen men . . . We have a real problem."

"Standing by," Vargas said.

Boxer keyed all of the section chiefs and told them to take their orders only from him and to humor Bush.

"We must sail to Australia," Bush said. "That's our only hope.

Boxer keyed the helmsman. "Take whatever course Captain Bush orders."

"Aye, aye, Skipper," the helmsman answered.

"Commander Lowe to the bridge, on the double," Bush said.

Cynthia looked questioningly at Boxer.

"Well doc, what do we do?" Boxer asked.

"Let her go," the MO answered. "I doubt if he will molest her on the bridge. He probably wants to show her that he now commands the *Turtle*."

"Can you cope with it?" Boxer asked, looking at Cynthia.

"I'll try," she said in a frightened voice.

"Commander Lowe," Bush said over the MC, "to the bridge, on the double."

"Go," Boxer said.

Cynthia nodded, stood up and walked quickly out of the cabin.

Boxer keyed Vargas. "Can you get someone in position to cover Bush with a rifle?"

"Negative, Skipper. I already thought of that and took a look."

"Gas?"

"Only as a last resort," Vargas answered. "If you use it, we'll have to surface immediately and vent the entire boat. He has us by the short hairs. By the way, just in case you haven't already guessed, he's armed."

"I guessed," Boxer answered.

"Bet you can't guess with what?"

"This isn't the time for guessing games."

"The old service issue .45," Vargas said.

"That's not what I wanted to hear," Boxer said.

"Sorry, Skipper . . . Ten four."

"We've got to end this," Boxer said, "before someone is killed."

Bush came on the MC again. "Now hear this . . . All hands now hear this . . . Commander Lowe is on the bridge with me . . . Alright Commander, the penalty for being a whore is to be a whore . . . Now what I want you to do is take off your clothing . . . That's right . . . I want you to strip . . . And one by one you'll fuck each man I call to the bridge . . . But I will begin the punishment . . . Now strip!"

Boxer keyed Vargas. "Use the gas!"

"Aye, aye, Skipper," Vargas answered.

Boxer keyed the DO. "Head for the surface . . . No

221

signals. Go!"

The *Turtle* broke water eight minutes later. Vargas and his men secured the bridge two minutes after that.

Boxer, protected with a gas mask, rushed to the bridge, switched on the MC and ordered all hatches open and all blowers on. Then he looked at Cowly, who lay gagging on the deck with Bush and Cynthia.

"Medics to the bridge," he said on the MC. "Medics to the bridge on the double." Then he keyed MO. "Keep Bush sedated . . . I don't want a repeat performance . . . Let me know the conditions of Commander Lowe and Cowly."

"Aye, aye, Skipper," the MO said.

Boxer keyed the DCO. "I'm going to stop all engines. Get your men over the side and have them look at that drive shaft seal."

"Aye, aye, Skipper," the DCO reported.

Boxer activated the outside bridge from the COM-COMP and immediately transferred operations to it. He keyed the EO. "Stop all engines."

"Stopping all engines," the EO said.

The *Turtle* began to lose forward momentum and soon was dead in the water.

Boxer watched the damage control men go off the stern. From time to time, he looked up at the beautiful blue sky and wondered how many aircraft that he couldn't see, or their radar couldn't pick up, had spotted the *Turtle* and had reported its position.

The MO keyed Boxer. "Skipper, Commander Lowe and Cowly are fine . . . Cowly needed five stitches on the back of his head . . . Bush struck him with the .45. He'll have a headache for a few days, but nothing else is wrong with him."

"Roger that," Boxer said.

It took slightly more than an hour for the *Turtle* to be completely vented.

Just as Boxer was getting ready to order the Damage Control Team back on bord, the DCO keyed him. "Skipper, the seal was damaged by the net we had to cut away. She'll hold though for anything less than five zero zero feet."

"Are you sure about the depth?" Boxer asked.

"It's a good guesstimate . . . Especially if I use HP air to back it."

"Roger that," Boxer answered and hit the klaxon three times. "All hands," he said over the MC, "Clear the deck . . . Clear the bridge . . . Stand by to dive . . . Stand by to dive . . . Stand by to dive."

Moments later the *Turtle* slipped beneath the sun drenched surface of the Mediterranean.

Sixteen

Under cover of darkness, the *Turtle* entered the cove in the Gulf of Sidra.

Boxer was at the COMCOMP. The UWIS was on. "Mahony," he said, "zero eight degrees to the port."

"Zero eight to port," Mahony answered.

Boxer keyed the EO. "Fourteen hundred rpms."

"Going to fourteen hundred rpms," the EO answered.

Boxer felt every muscle in his body tighten. He switched on the MC. "Stand by for beaching . . . Stand by for beaching." Suddenly the *Turtle* ground against the bottom. Boxer was almost unseated. "Cowly, lower treads."

"Aye, aye, Skipper," Cowly answered.

Boxer keyed the EO. "Transfer power to treads."

"Power being transferred," the EO said.

His throat dry, Boxer eased the throttle forward. The *Turtle* groaned; then started to climb up the slope of the underwater beach. Boxer eyed the overhead depth gauge. They were coming to thirty feet. He eased the throttle back. The *Turtle* slowed then stopped.

Boxer looked up at Cowly, who wore a bandage around his head, and said, "So far so good."

"One hour to jump off time," Cowly said.

Boxer was going to ask if everyone involved in the assault knew his assignment, but in the last ten hours every man had gone over his particular function dozens of times. Vargas was going to attack from the front. Bruno would attack through the tunnels, and a third team, under the command of Captain Stevens, would go for the radar station; then he and his men would cover the withdrawal of the other two teams.

There was nothing complex about the scheme. Its success depended on the element of surprise.

Boxer keyed Vargas. "Stand by to enter exitbay."

"Standing by," Vargas answered.

"Enter exitbay," Boxer ordered and he activated the TV cameras that gave him a picture of the area.

The assault teams were filing into the area. Each man carried the new M-38 rifle, five grenades, a .357 magnum, a .32 caliber automtic, a trench knife and other assorted gear, including first aid equipment and two lethal tablets in case they were captured. Each man knew that if he were captured, he'd be tortured until he revealed everything he knew about the *Turtle*; then he'd be killed.

Vargas keyed Boxer from one of the assault vehicles. "Ready to go, Skipper."

"Roger that," Boxer answered and he keyed Bruno. "Ready?"

"Ready, Skipper," Bruno answered.

Boxer switched on the MC. "Sanchez to the bridge . . . Sanchez to the bridge."

The SO keyed Boxer. "Skipper, there's some sort of surface disturbance."

"Roger that," Boxer said and relayed the information to Vargas and Bruno.

"Probably the wind," Bruno answered. "Strong winds come off the desert at this time of the year."

"Roger that," Boxer answered and saw Sanchez coming up to the bridge. "I thought you'd want to be here during the assault."

"Yes, thank you," Sanchez answered.

225

Boxer ran SYSCHEK. All systems were green. He keyed Bruno. "Are you ready to move out?"

"Ready," Bruno answered.

Boxer switched on the MC. "Stand by to flood exit bay . . . All hands, remember we'll be heavy in the bow. . . ." He turned to Cowly. "Flood the bay."

"Aye, aye, Skipper," Cowly answered.

Boxer turned his attention to the TV monitor. The water rushed in from six different points: each of the four corners; then center and the bow. Everything was working perfectly, just as it had during the one practice run off Corsica just ten hours ago.

"Bay one third full," Cowly reported.

"Take a look," Boxer said.

Cowly moved over to the COMCOMP. "I wouldn't want to be there, or where they're going," he commented.

"Neither would I," Sanchez said.

Boxer didn't say anything. His inclination was to be where the action was. But he had to stay with the *Turtle*.

Cowly returned to his duty station.

Boxer keyed Bruno. "Good luck," he said.

"Thanks," Bruno answered. "But it will be a piece of cake."

"Bay completely flooded," Cowly said.

"Open ramp doors," Boxer responded.

"Aye, aye, Skipper," Cowly answered.

As soon as the opening in the bow of the *Turtle* was wide enough to allow a man to pass through it, Bruno moved his men out. He took the lead.

Boxer turned his attention to the UWIS. He could only see them for a short time, before they vanished into the inky blackness of the water.

"How long before they reach their position?" Sanchez asked.

"Twenty minutes, if they don't encounter any

opposition," Boxer answered. He was tempted to call Bruno on the radio. But he himself had ordered that radio communication between the *Turtle* and the assault teams be absolutely limited, especially during the landing and withdrawal operations.

The SO keyed Boxer. "Skipper, that surface disturbance seems to be concentrated at the mouth of the cove."

"Roger that," Boxer answered. "See if you can get some better definition on it."

"Ten four," the SO responded.

Boxer watched the clock. The minutes ticked by.

Bruno keyed Boxer. "Position," he said, using one word to indicate that he was in position.

Boxer answered with the word, "Company." This meant that the other teams were on their way. He watched Vargas's three armoured vehicles move out and Stevens's team follow. He switched off the TV monitor and the UWIS. "Now all we have to do is wait," Boxer said.

"Skipper, Commander Lowe requests permission to come to the bridge," Cowly said.

"Permission granted," Boxer answered.

To ease the tightness in his neck, Boxer moved his head from side to side.

"Coffee, Skipper?" Cowly asked.

"Sure, why not," Boxer answered.

Cowly called down to the Mess Chief and asked for four coffees and four pieces of cake.

Cynthia came onto the bridge. "I request permission to remain here during the course of the action," she said.

Boxer hesitated. "It could become very, very hectic," he said.

"I'll keep out of the way, I promise," Cynthia said; then she added, "I might not ever get another chance like this."

227

Boxer nodded.

One of the men from the galley brought up a tray of coffee and slices of pie and cake.

Boxer drank the coffee and nibbled at a piece of pound cake. He ran another SYSCHEK. All systems were green.

"Vargas and Stevens should be in position by now," Boxer commented. Almost as soon as he finished speaking, both men reported that they were in position.

"Go," Boxer radioed. "And good luck!"

Boxer stood up and began to walk about the bridge; then he stopped, touched his toes several times and did a few deep knee bends before he returned to the COMCOMP.

"Can we hear them?" Sanchez asked.

"It's really worse if you do," Boxer answered. "But if you want to, I'll tune to the frequency they're using." He adjusted several dials. "We'll hear it on the bridge," Boxer explained, "but the rest of the boat won't." He looked at Cowly. Cynthia was standing near him.

Suddenly he heard Stevens say, "Keep firing . . . Keep firing . . . Spic . . . Meeting heavy opposition . . . Meeting heavy opposition."

"I hear ya," Vargas answered. "Taking casualties . . . Taking casualties . . . Scout," he said, using Bruno's code name, "what's your situation?"

"Bruno isn't answering!" Sanchez exclaimed.

Vargas repeated his question.

"He still doesn't answer," Sanchez said.

"Maybe he can't receive or send in the caves?" Cowly suggested. He put down his container of coffee and joined Boxer at the COMCOMP.

"Scout," Vargas said, "we're in trouble . . . Need your help."

The SO keyed Boxer. "Skipper, ID'd the disturbance."

"Can't it hold?" Boxer asked.

"Skipper, a net has been pulled across the mouth of

228

the cove," the SO said.

"What the hell are you talking about?" Boxer questioned.

"Switch on the scope," the SO told him.

Boxer reached over and turned on the Sonar scope. "Got it."

"That smudge means that there's a steel net out there," the SO said.

"Roger that," Boxer answered. He looked at Cowly. "We've got to get the hell out of here . . . We've been set up." He switched on the MC. "All hands stand by . . . All hands stand by . . . This is an emergency. We are abandoning this position . . . We are abandoning this position."

Boxer keyed the EO. "Full power on treads."

"Full power on treads," the EO answered.

"Vent bay area," Boxer told Cowly.

Boxer shifted the treads' drive into reverse and slowly eased the power throttle forward. The *Turtle* began to crawl backwards.

"Casualties heavy," Vargas said.

Boxer keyed him. "Point two," he said. "Abandon mission. Point two . . . Abandon mission . . . Point two."

"Ten four," Vargas answered. "We've been had."

Boxer contacted Stevens. "Break off engagement . . . Point two."

"Ten four," Stevens answered.

Boxer watched the depth gauge. They were in sixty feet of water.

Suddenly an explosion burst over the *Turtle*. The lights dimmed; then came back on.

Boxer switched on the MC. "Report damage," he barked.

All reports were negative.

Boxer slowed the portside tread and the *Turtle* began to turn toward the mouth of the cove.

Two more depth charges exploded above the *Turtle*. One struck the deck before it detonated.

Boxer keyed the EO. "Lose some oil."

"Aye, aye, Skipper," the EO answered.

"How are you going to get past the net?" Sanchez asked. His face was ashen.

"Blow it out of the water," Boxer answered.

"Can't make point two," Stevens radioed. "Going down for the count."

"Holy Christ!" Cowly exclaimed.

Boxer gritted his teeth.

Another explosion crashed down in front of the *Turtle*.

"Check the bay area," Boxer said.

"Secure," Cowly answered after a few moments.

Boxer keyed the EO. "Stand by to transfer power to drive shafts."

"Standing by," the EO answered.

Boxer eased the throttle back. The *Turtle* stopped. He keyed the DO. "Make seven zero feet."

"Making seven zero feet," the DO answered.

As soon as the depth gauge shows a rise of one zero feet, Boxer said to Cowly, "Retract treads."

"Aye, aye, Skipper," Cowly answered.

Boxer motioned to Cynthia. "Plug in the earphone over there and monitor Vargas."

"Aye, aye, Skipper," she answered in a low voice.

Boxer keyed the EO. "Transfer power to drive shafts."

"Transferring power," the EO answered.

"Make one zero knots," Boxer said.

"Making one zero knots," the EO answered.

Boxer switched on the MC. "All hands now hear this . . . All hands now hear this . . . I need four volunteers to attach explosive charges to a steel net that's blocking our escape . . . Unless that net is blown we don't stand much chance of getting out of the cove alive."

In a matter of minutes, two junior officers and several enlisted men came to the bridge. Boxer nodded and said, "There's a real kicker in this . . . Those that go are going to have to hitch a ride on the outside of the *Turtle* until we can bring them in and that might mean being out there for several hours."

None of the men moved.

"Mr. Cowly tear up some paper, mark four pieces with an x and leave the other pieces blank . . . The men who pull the x's go."

"Aye, aye, Skipper," Cowly answered.

Boxer keyed the EO. "Go to zero five knots."

"Going to zero five knots," the EO answered.

"What I don't understand," Sanchez said, "is why they really don't clobber us?"

"Why should they? They have us . . . I think they think they've trapped a standard submarine . . . They probably know it's an American submarine . . . But I don't think they have any idea of what we are."

"Where are depth charges coming from?"

"'Copters, probably."

The SO keyed Boxer. "Target . . . Bearing three two degrees . . . Range eight thousand yards . . . Speed two two knots . . . ID the *Skorky Class Destroyer*."

"Roger that," Boxer said. That was a 1960 vintage Russian destroyer. Many of them were sold to Mideastern and African countries.

"Skipper," Cowly said, "the four men have been chosen."

Boxer turned toward Cowly. "Each man in a scuba with enough air in his tanks to sustain him for five hours and armed with a knife and the standard underwater rifle. They will slip a torpedo out of its tube and attach it to the net and we will detonate it from the bridge."

"Any questions?" Cowly asked.

Each of the men shook his head.

"Get going," Boxer told them.

"Skipper," Cynthia said. "Vargas hasn't transmitted for the last ten minutes."

"Did you try to raise him?"

Cynthia nodded.

"Keep trying," Boxer said tightly.

Boxer turned to Sanchez. "They sure as hell knew we were coming."

Sanchez nodded.

"Skipper, the men are in the exit chamber," Cowly said.

"Roger that," Boxer said and he keyed the TO. "Load a torpedo in tube number one . . . Prepare for remote detonation . . . Open torpedo door . . . The torpedo will be removed by four of our men."

"Aye, aye, Skipper," the TO answered.

Boxer checked the position of the *Turtle* relative to the net. Three hundred yards separated them. He waited until it was down to two hundred yards before he keyed the EO and said, "Stop all engines."

"Stopping all engines."

Boxer turned to Cowly. "Flood exit chamber."

"Exit chamber flooding," Cowly said.

The SO keyed Boxer. "Target changing course . . . Bearing forty five degress . . . Range six thousand yards . . . Speed two two knots."

"Roger that," Boxer said. "It's going to watch-dog out there."

"Ten four," the SO answered.

"DEMO-team out," Cowly said.

Boxer checked the COMCOMP. The red indication light flashed.

"Close door and vent chamber," Boxer said.

"Aye, aye, Skipper," Cowly answered.

Boxer checked the digital clock. It was only 04:15.

There was at least an hour and half before the sun came up.

The TO keyed Boxer. "Fish ready and waiting in tube one."

"Roger that," Boxer said, switching on the UWIS. He watched the men slip the torpedo from the tube and work it toward the net less than a hundred yards away.

"Skipper, Vargas says he'll try to make point two," Cynthia said.

Boxer nodded. "At least he's still alive," he said.

The ranking officer on the DEMO team keyed Boxer. "Fish in place."

"Roger that," Boxer answered. "Start back toward us."

"Ten four," the man answered.

Boxer keyed the EO. "Twelve hundred rpms."

"Aye, aye, Skipper."

The *Turtle* began to ease forward.

"Helmsman, zero five degrees."

"Zero five degrees," Mahony answered.

Suddenly two explosions hammered down on the *Turtle*'s bow, forcing it to drop several feet.

Boxer checked the UWIS. "Gone!" he exclaimed. "The four of them are gone!" Suddenly he saw the head of one of the men float by. The mask plate was shattered. He pursed his lips and looked away.

"Are you alright, Skipper?" Cowly asked.

Boxer nodded, found his voice and said, "Prepare to detonate."

"Aye, aye, Skipper," Cowly said.

Boxer keyed the EO. "As soon as you hear the explosion, I want full power."

"Aye, aye, Skipper," the EO answered.

Boxer keyed the DO. "Make eighty feet."

"Making eighty feet," the DO answered.

Boxer keyed the TO. "Load tubes one and two . . . Arm torpedos."

"Arming torpedos one and two," the TO answered.

"All FC data on AUTO . . . Set to fire at six thousand yards . . . COMCOMP control."

"Aye, aye, Skipper," the TO answered.

Boxer ran a last minute SYSCHEK. All systems were green. He turned toward Cowly. "Fire," he said in a low voice.

Cowly nodded and pushed the remote fire control button.

An enormous explosion rolled over the *Turtle*. The next instant she lurched forward and met the shock wave with her bow. For an instant she seemed to hesitate; then she pushed through it.

The SO keyed Boxer. "The net broke apart!"

"Roger that," Boxer said.

Boxer looked at the UWIS screen. They were out of the cove. He keyed the SO. "Transmit target INFO to FC computer."

"Ten four."

The TO keyed Boxer. "One five seconds to firing . . . One zero seconds . . . Zero five seconds . . . One away . . . Two away."

Boxer hit the stop watch. He watched the torpedos on the UWIS. The first one caught the destroyer mid-ship. The explosion tore the hull in half. The second fish struck the bow section and blew it apart.

"Helmsman, turn to course four eight degrees," Boxer said.

"Coming to course four eight degrees," the helmsman answered.

Boxer switched on the MC. "Now hear this . . . Now hear this . . . We are going to attempt to rescue some of our men . . . All section chiefs allow three men at a time to go to the mess area . . . We're going to catch a lot of fire . . . All hands remain at General Quarters."

"Skipper," Cynthia said, "Vargas reports six survivors including himself . . . He says they're waiting for you at Point Two."

"Tell him to swim out to us . . . We can wait off shore—"

"The transmission has suddenly stopped, Skipper," Cynthia said softly. "I'm sorry."

Boxer switched on the radio. There was nothing but static. He pursed his lips, and fighting down a sob, he said, "Helmsman come to course three six zero degrees."

"Coming to course three six zero degrees," Mahony answered.

Boxer looked toward Cowly. "I can't risk the boat and the men on the off chance the Spic is still alive."

Cowly nodded.

Boxer keyed the COMMO. "Send the following message to carrier group SHIELD: Coming into your zone. ETA zero eleven hundred hours. Bogies will probably be close behind. Send up air screen.

"And send the following message to Headquarters and to Admiral Stark. "Mission failed; they were waiting for us." Boxer's voice broke. He took a moment to clear his throat and continued. "All assault forces either killed or captured." Boxer took a deep breath. "Send it . . . Send the fucking message!"

"Aye, aye, Skipper," the COMMO answered.

Boxer uttered a ragged sigh, stood up and began to pace. Except for the worrying sound of the air blowers, the bridge was silent.

Boxer pursed his lips. He felt as if there was an enormous weight pushing down on him. That some of the men ashore might be alive was a possibility. He stopped and looked at Cowly; then at Cynthia.

Neither of them met his gaze.

"The odds are against any of them being alive," Boxer

235

said aloud.

Everyone remained silent.

Boxer returned to the COMCOMP and sat down. There was no way he could abandon Vargas or any of the other men. "Okay," he said after a few minutes. "We're going back. Maybe we'll be lucky. But even if we are we're going to have to fight our way in and out. And this time you can bet the Libyans will have their Ruskie friends to help them."

ASHES
by William W. Johnstone

OUT OF THE ASHES (1137, $3.50)

Ben Raines hadn't looked forward to the War, but he knew it was coming. After the balloons went up, Ben was one of the survivors, fighting his way across the country, searching for his family, and leading a band of new pioneers attempting to bring America OUT OF THE ASHES.

FIRE IN THE ASHES (1310, $3.50)

It's 1999 and the world as we know it no longer exists. Ben Raines, leader of the Resistance, must regroup his rebels and prep them for bloody guerilla war. But are they ready to face an even fiercer foe—the human mutants threatening to overpower the world!

ANARCHY IN THE ASHES (1387, $3.50)

Out of the smoldering nuclear wreckage of World War III, Ben Raines has emerged as the strong leader the Resistance needs. When Sam Hartline, the mercenary, joins forces with an invading army of Russians, Ben and his people raise a bloody banner of defiance to defend earth's last bastion of freedom.

BLOOD IN THE ASHES (1537, $3.50)

As Raines and his ragged band of followers search for land that has escaped radiation, the insidious group known as The Ninth Order rises up to destroy them. In a savage battle to the death, it is the fate of America itself that hangs in the balance!

Available wherever paperbacks are sold, or order direct from the Publisher. Send cover price plus 50¢ per copy for mailing and handling to Zebra Books, Dept. 1769, 475 Park Avenue South, New York, N.Y. 10016. DO NOT SEND CASH.

THE NEWEST ADVENTURES AND ESCAPADES OF BOLT
by Cort Martin

THE WORLD-AT-WAR SERIES
by Lawrence Cortesi

COUNTDOWN TO PARIS   (1548, $3.25)

Having stormed the beaches of Normandy, every GI had one dream: to liberate Paris from the Nazis. Trapping the enemy in the Falaise Pocket, the Allies would shatter the powerful German 7th Army Group, opening the way for the . . . COUNTDOWN TO PARIS.

GATEWAY TO VICTORY   (1496, $3.25)

After Leyte, the U.S. Navy was at the threshold of Japan's Pacific Empire. With his legendary cunning, Admiral Halsey devised a brilliant plan to deal a crippling blow in the South China Sea to Japan's military might.

ROMMEL'S LAST STAND   (1415, $3.25)

In April of 1943 the Nazis attempted a daring airlift of supplies to a desperate Rommel in North Africa. But the Allies were lying in wait for one of the most astonishing and bloody air victories of the war.

LAST BRIDGE TO VICTORY   (1393, $3.25)

Nazi troops had blown every bridge on the Rhine, stalling Eisenhower's drive for victory. In one final blood-soaked battle, the fanatic resistance of the Nazis would test the courage of every American soldier.

PACIFIC SIEGE   (1363, $3.25)

If the Allies failed to hold New Guinea, the entire Pacific would fall to the Japanese juggernaut. For six brutal months they drenched the New Guinea jungles with their blood, hoping to live to see the end of the . . . PACIFIC SIEGE.

THE BATTLE FOR MANILA   (1334, $3.25)

A Japanese commander's decision—against orders—to defend Manila to the death led to the most brutal combat of the entire Pacific campaign. A living hell that was . . . THE BATTLE FOR MANILA.

Available wherever paperbacks are sold, or order direct from the Publisher. Send cover price plus 50¢ per copy for mailing and handling to Zebra Books, Dept. 1769, 475 Park Avenue South, New York, N.Y. 10016. DO NOT SEND CASH.